# SOULSTICE

## Alyx's Story

A companion novella to *SOULED*

Soulstice is a work of fiction. The events and characters described herein are imaginary and are not intended to refer to specific living persons or experiences. The business and locations, however, are in Sandpoint, Idaho, and are only included in this novel as locales and have not endorsed the opinions/imagination of the author.

The opinions expressed in this fictional piece are solely the opinion of the author. The author has represented and warranted full ownership and/or legal right to publish all materials in this book.

# FROM BAD TO WORSE

How the two of them ever got to the point of falling in love, I'll never understand. The differences between my mom and dad eventually yawned into an abyss so wide and so deep that it threatened to swallow the family. My mom never stopped trying to keep it together. She pretended to believe in my dad's church and what it stood for. She even went as far as to perform her rituals in secret. Honestly, though, it did no good. It was like trying to stop an avalanche from pouring down a mountain, because Dad knew her façade was all bullshit. He openly resented the fact that she refused to give up her Wicca practice and fought back in his own screwed up way.

For as long as I could remember, Dad had spent more time in bars than with us, holding his worn-out Bible with one hand and taking shots of whiskey with the other. He emptied our bank account faster than he and my mom could fill it. She did the best she could to budget our money, but Dad's spending habits were hard to keep up with.

So, to bring in extra cash, Mom made candles and sage bundles and sold them to the neighbors. Certain that the scented candles were somehow tainted with evil spirits, my father forbid her to burn them in the den, which was the one room in the house that needed the scent of a candle the most. The sickly stench of stale alcohol saturated the walls and blanketed the furniture and carpet. I was too embarrassed to have anyone over to my house. I never knew when or what shape Dad would be in when he came home, but more often than not, he would pass out in the den after hours of drinking. I couldn't bear the thought of anyone seeing him like that.

People in small towns like ours talked too much about everyone's business but their own.

Imagine opening up a box and never knowing what was going to be inside. That's what my childhood was like. Rainbows and unicorns one day and gargantuan tarantulas the next. I'd withdraw into my shell for days on end, preferring my own head space to the rocky footing of my life.

But Mom was always looking out for me. She taught me to look for the consistency outside my window - the simple concepts, things I could count on - like the perfection of the seasons and the cycles of the moon. She let me watch her perform rituals and taught me simple manipulations of the elements, things that could be duplicated over and over.

Back then I was in a hurry to grow up so I could do the rituals on my own. At ten years old, I wanted to be just like her. Skilled and talented. Unwavering in my faith. Steady and strong.

But at the first real, serious test, at the moment where maturity, skill, and levelheadedness were needed, I failed.

Horribly.

After that, my mom no longer had the burden of hiding our practices from my dad – for a couple reasons.

One, I ran from everything she taught me, by tucking my budding talent into the darkest corners of my mind, hoping it would never be discovered.

Two, Dad was dead.

# CHAPTER ONE

After Dad died, staying in the obscure, Bible-thumping town in Illinois where I was born wasn't an option. We'd lost our home and we had no friends to speak of. Our only family was Aunt Sarah, who lived a few hours away.

We packed the car with what little we had and drove across the country, leaving behind the life we'd known, along with memories of Dad. A yellow highlighted line snaked its way across the grids of the map and settled in Sandpoint, Idaho. I had no idea why Mom had chosen there, of all places. Wasn't one town just as bad as the other? I only knew the name of Sandpoint through a few discussions I'd overheard between my mom and Aunt Sarah when she would visit. Aunt Sarah said there was something special about that particular town. Something about a bridge. Something about a vortex or Christ grid.

Whatever the reason, I didn't care. As long as it took us far from the life that was never normal, away from a life that had me living in the shadows, afraid of the next fight that would have my brother, Jesse, and me hiding.

"Mom?"

"Hmm?" She'd stopped humming along to the Rolling Stones that played on the stereo and waited for me to talk.

"Are Jesse and I going to have to work?"

Seeing how we barely scraped by in Illinois with both parents working, I was afraid we'd be living on the streets.

Her soft laugh was both surprising and comforting.

"No, honey. You don't need to worry. I have that taken care of."

It turned out that Mom had money – a lot of it. As we drove across the long stretches of Wyoming toward our new home, Mom told us that when my grandparents died sixteen years earlier, they'd left her a big, fat trust fund. She'd kept it secret from my dad, hiring a financial firm to manage it, so he wouldn't blow all the money.

Passing through Coeur d'Alene on our way to Sandpoint, I started to feel better about the move. Having Silverwood, a theme park, so close to Sandpoint, definitely trumped the deal.

Our lives were definitely going to be different. I knew it in my heart – no, in my soul – because in the time it took us to drive the almost two miles across the Long Bridge, the bridge that spanned the lake between Sandpoint and the small town of Sagle, there was a palpable shift in the air that threatened to slice through the lock on my packed-away past. There was something intense about this area and it froze me up as if I'd jumped head-first into a snow bank. That was the moment I decided: this was a new town, and there was going to be a new me. I had a plan.

~ ~ ~

The Power Ranger theme song chimed from my cell. Okay. So I'm a bit of a geek.

"You've got a text," I said in my best AOL guy voice.

*Alyx! HELLO! What time u gonna b here? Itz 3!*

Taylor, my best friend, hated that I was always late to her parties. In my defense, I was never *intentionally* late. I just had a hard time finding motivation to rush over there when she wanted me to. I'd always go, but would come home from those parties feeling wiped out, as if I had walked through an energy vacuum. I tried to find common ground, but could never seem to connect with anyone.

*Getting in shower now*, I texted back, even though *now* wasn't really *now*, as in this moment now. I tossed the cell on the bed. I could almost hear her stomp her foot with impatience, a gesture that used to be endearing, but over the last three years, it'd gotten a little irritating.

Taylor had been my best friend since freshman year when we met at Sandpoint High's orientation. I remembered the electric blue iridescent color on her fingernails and she loved the candy-apple-green shade I coated mine with that morning. Taylor was fun and she made me laugh – something no one had been able to do for a long time. We'd been inseparable since then, sharing clothes and secrets. We even looked alike, except my blonde hair was a little darker than hers. Our tastes ran surprisingly similar on a lot of things – including boys. Whenever we liked the same boy, though, I'd back down so she could have an open playing field. I was always afraid that being close to a guy meant letting him get too close to my past. And if I was going to do that, he'd better be the right one.

I didn't bother looking at the phone when *Go, Go, Power Rangers* chimed in. I knew it would be Taylor telling me to hurry. It was so typical of her. Instead, I picked up the deck of oracle cards that I'd been shuffling earlier. My mom put this particular deck on my bed a few days earlier with no explanation, but I didn't need one. I knew what she was up to. She was trying to draw me out of my world and back into hers. She dropped subtle hints, bought me cards and pendants, and nudged me in the direction of reconnecting with my elemental senses. Although I appreciated what she was trying to do, I wasn't buying into it and I didn't know if I ever would. She knew I struggled with coming to terms with my past. I'd cut metaphysics out of my life because to me, that had been the root of our problems. For the last few years I stood firm in my decision to be a *normal* teen and connecting with my guides wasn't part of the plan.

The cards felt awkward in my hands and my fingers were clumsy. I didn't even know why I bothered with them. I made a half-hearted effort to focus while shuffling the cards, but gave up when a card caught the edge of another, did a flutter flip, and landed on my lap. I flipped the corner of the oracle card up with my freshly painted pinky nail. The card was *"Release"* and was symbolized by a beautiful woman, elven-like, with shimmering midnight blue hair, the hem of her pale-green gown raised slightly as if carried on a breeze. Her hands released multi-colored leaves to the wind and she stared at me with a strange, captivating mix of both sadness and hope in her violet eyes.

My heart lurched. I never considered myself compassionate, especially towards a stranger. Concerned, perhaps, but to feel an actual ache for what I saw in this woman's eyes had me, well, kind of freaked out.

I opened the instruction book and found the page that explained the meaning of this card. After speed-reading the paragraph three times, I realized I wasn't absorbing a single word on the page. Partly because I didn't want to tap into the wisdom of the cards, and partly because I was supposed to be getting ready for a party. Mostly, though, because the weight of the emotion hung around my neck and threatened to choke me.

"Release?" I asked the card, quickly forming my own interpretation of it to deflect the effects of her stare. "I'll release all right." I gathered the cards and explanation book and tossed them onto the bed before standing up.

I had more important pursuits than analyzing my past, present, and future. This summer there was some serious socializing to do.

~ ~ ~

A few houses away from Taylor's, I parked behind
Justin Coon's truck. Compared to his Nissan, my Audi
was pretentious, and very shallow, especially for this
area, but it helped create the image I wanted. The makeup
and clothes we wore, the money we flashed around, are
either a fortress around or a window to our soul. I'd
chosen my image to be an armor to hide the fact that I
was the daughter of an alcoholic. As time went on, I
hoped that image would stick and Justin would be drawn
to the illusion that I created: a well-off party girl. I was
still waiting for him to notice.

I took a cigarette and a lighter out of my purse and
shouldered open the door. Leaning against my car, I lit
up, giving me a few minutes before going inside. Had I
known Justin would be at the party, I might not have
shown up at all. He obviously wasn't interested in me.
Why I still bothered to think about him anymore was
beyond me, but just like smoking, pining after Justin was
a nasty habit that would be hard to break.

In our freshman year, when Taylor and I first noticed
him, he sat in front of us at a football game. There was
one of those moments I read about in teen novels when
the girl can't freakin' breathe when she sees the guy. That
was me. Of course, Taylor was all into him, too. She kept
nudging me, asking me what she should say.

She finally quit poking me when the cheerleaders
walked in front of the bleachers, throwing candy and t-
shirts up into the stands. Like everyone else, Taylor
yelled, trying to get their attention. The cheerleaders
launched a rolled-up shirt our way and dozens of hands
rose in response – right along with mine. From the
moment it left the cheerleader's fingertips, as it sailed
over and through the hands that shot up to intercept it, I

9

focused on the shirt. It was mine, but my concentration shattered when it grazed someone's fingertips and broke its path to me. Justin's hands got caught up in the mix and for a few seconds it was just the two of us, fighting for control. I don't know why I was trying so hard to grab it. I mean, it's not like I wore t-shirts or anything. Maybe it was because Justin wanted it. Maybe fighting for it would get his attention. Whatever the reason, I leaned hard against his shoulder, pushing him down and out of the way, giving me the edge I needed to snatch it out of his hands.

"Oh, my God, Alyx! You're so lucky!" Taylor half smiled, half pouted at the prize I held against my chest.

But the victory was hollow. I wanted Justin's attention way more than I wanted a stupid shirt I'd never wear. I tapped him on the shoulder, and when he turned those hazel eyes on me, my insides melted.

"Here," I said, shoving the rolled up fabric into his hand, "It'd look better on you."

He looked at me for a couple of seconds as if trying to remember my face, then shrugged. "No, you keep it." He turned back around. That was that.

My one and only close encounter with him and he shut me down. He was so nice about it, which took the sting out of the rejection, but unfortunately made me like him more.

I dropped the cigarette on the street and ground my shoe over it, squashing it along with the memories of that night. Even as I ceremoniously scooped up the cigarette and tossed it into the trash bag in the back seat of my car, I knew that no matter how many times I tried to obliterate the feelings I had, it was useless to try to forget Justin.

*Ugh.* It totally sucked liking someone who didn't like me back. It was his brooding nature and the intensity that he cared for his friends, mostly Seth Thompson, that drew me in. He was deep. He'd be the type who thought things through before making a choice. No snap decisions with that guy. He wasn't like all the other testosterone-driven horn-dogs who walked the school halls. Damn, and he was hot. Being on the wrestling team definitely had its positive physical benefits. Looking at him was enough to make my heart do back-flips and my stomach turn into a butterfly sanctuary.

I'd have to get over that.

Starting tomorrow.

I ran my fingers over the shiny black paint of my car before dragging them across the faded red of his truck. Justin and I weren't so different, really. He was popular. I was popular. We both liked sports. He was on the wrestling team and, well, I liked to watch him wrestle. If only I had the nerve to go after him. But I wouldn't do well with another rejection. Besides, Taylor still liked him.

I blew wisps of hair off my forehead with a quick breath and rearranged the ends of my hair to fall over my shoulders. I pulled down on the hem of my shorts and adjusted my cami for optimal attraction. If I could get him to look my way, I'd be happy with that. And if he actually talked to me, I'd be ecstatic. I wouldn't fight for him, but if *he* came after *me*, that'd be totally different. I definitely wouldn't turn him away – Taylor or no Taylor. Who was I to waste a good opportunity?

The moment I pushed open the front door of her house, the loud buzz of voices and music wrapped around me. It drew me in, towards the kitchen where a humongous buffet was laid out on the central island. Half the guys circling the food were on the wrestling team and the other half was the football team. Beyond that, outside on the patio, Nate, a nerdy-looking guy with a great sense of musical style, acted as DJ for the party. I got a few 'sups and more than a few stares from the boys as I passed them on my way to the back of the house.

11

Through the sliding glass doors leading to the backyard, I caught a glimpse of Justin by the coolers that lined the fence.

I always thought Justin was one of the most perfect guys in school, with the right balance of confidence and humility, brains and brawn. I loved the way his dusty blonde hair fell over his hazel eyes, but my favorite part of his face to stare at was his amazingly kissable lips. The perfect shape, the perfect fullness. Perfect for mine.

Even though he never went out of his way to talk to me, he was always extremely polite when we passed in the halls or saw each other at the store or library. Not that it made me feel any better, but it seemed he was like that toward all females. He laughed easily when he was with his friends, but when he was around girls, not so much. He kept them at arm's length and rarely got into too much discussion. And if he ever did get cornered into talking, he'd close off a bit and back away as if he'd rather not be seen together.

Except when he was with Dani, Seth's girlfriend. He seemed different around her - smiling more, laughing more. His personal space disappeared when she stood next to him. That was the Justin I'd like to know. That was the Justin I dreamed of.

Drawing in a deep breath, I stepped outside and headed in his direction, thinking that getting a soda was as good an excuse as any to get close to him.

His attention broke from Travis, one of the guys on the football team, and he glanced up. Our eyes locked for a second, and in that second I saw… nothing. Not a spark of interest. Nada. Someone might as well have sliced my heart open - along with my ego. If it weren't for his quick, almost shy glance at my cleavage, I didn't exist to him. Par for the course.

*Hello? Alyx… this is your reality calling. When are you going to stop trying to be a part of his life?*

Snatching a soda out of a cooler, I turned and headed back inside. Maybe just a few more bleeding heart episodes and I'll give it up. Maybe I'll...

I heard Taylor's squeal before I saw her, but I wasn't ready for my arm to be almost yanked out of its socket.

"Alyx!" she pulled me into a hug. "Thanks for coming!" she said too loudly. Then her voice dropped to a whisper. "Can you believe he's here?"

"Who?" As if I didn't know. I turned and looked at Justin.

Her fingers pinched into my arm. "Don't look at him, Alyx. He'll think I'm talking about him." She dragged me deeper inside the house.

Yeah, like she wasn't already making a scene. "Have you said anything to him yet?" I asked.

"I said 'hi,' but he hasn't been here long enough for me to say much more." She dropped her hand to her side, pulling her smile down with it. "And I probably won't get another chance. He's always surrounded by his wrestling buddies *and* he'll be going to Hawaii for summer vacay."

She looked absolutely heartbroken. All through high school, Justin hadn't given her a second glance either, even though she was always up-front and in his face. She had some Justin radar system going on and she knew exactly where he was, like, all the time.

She spun around and proved me, once again, right on the money.

"See ya later, Justin!" she said. "Have a great time!" Like a flower to sunlight, Taylor's entire body came to life when he walked inside and passed us on the way to the front door.

"Yeah, thanks." He gave a very generic wave and stepped out the door, not even looking back.

Her shoulders slumped. I knew her pain only too well.

"Crap," Taylor muttered, punctuating it with a heavy sigh. "Come on. Let's get everybody dancing. That'll take my mind off him." She turned and walked toward the patio. She flipped her mood switch and signaled to Nate to crank up the music. Grabbing a guy named Caleb by the hand, she dragged him out on the patio and everyone followed, including me. Not because I wanted to dance, but, like Taylor, I needed a distraction - from everything.

Mom had been telling me for years that I was unique, that what I have is a gift, and that I should embrace, not hide, from it. But what if I didn't want to be unique? Maybe I didn't want to stand out. Unique wouldn't get me dates. Unique wouldn't keep Taylor and the others close in my orbit. And most definitely I wouldn't get the guy that I wanted, because he ran in a crowd like this one and the person I am inside would probably scare him away.

Devin Aster yanked me right out of my thoughts and straight against his chest.

"Hey, Alyx, dance with me."

I looked up at one of the other best-looking guys at the high school. I could hardly explain why Devin wanted to be with me. He was the prized, green-eyed, six-foot-tall star quarterback. I had him in a couple classes last year, but it wasn't like I talked to him all that much. Then again, I could hardly explain why I *didn't* want to be with him.

"Dance with me," he said again, lightly grinding his hips against me.

My first thought was to duck out of there and go home, but defeat won out. What did I have to lose? Justin wasn't around to notice or even care. The beat of the music was fast, urging my feet to kick it up, and still Devin pressed his body closer in a deliberate rhythm.

14

"Maybe we can hook up after the party," Devin said in a wickedly seductive whisper against my ear.

"Yeah. Maybe." I pulled back and smiled up at him. That should have been a dream come true. Devin was the only other guy I would consider hooking up with. Though he'd never be my first choice, second might just have to do.

# CHAPTER TWO

"You're home early." Jon, my step-dad, came out of the kitchen to greet me, drying his hands on a towel.

"Is everything okay?" Mom appeared behind him, her brows lifting slightly in question.

I definitely got my blues eyes from her. Dad's had been steely blue, and when turned on me, would cause my blood to freeze. Mom's were warm and soft, like a summer sky. Her physique would be considered small, especially standing next to Jon, who was almost a foot taller, but her personality was anything but that. Even when she didn't talk, her energy buzzed like crazed hummingbirds and filled a room with so much intensity, her vibes practically busted out the windows.

Jon and Mom had nice contrast and balance between the two of them: Mom's light brown hair, pale skin tone, and uncontainable energy against Jon's darker features, and maddeningly calm demeanor. They met at a retreat a few months after we moved to Sandpoint. He and my mom had gone there separately and came home as a couple. Jon was different than anyone she'd ever met before. The complete opposite of my unsupportive, suspicious, nail-to-the-cross dad, Jon not only encouraged my mom, he was her best student.

"Honey?" Mom brought me back.

"What?" I blinked my mind back into focus. "Oh, yeah. Everything is fine. I was bored."

"Hmm," she said, and headed for the dining table. She leaned over one of the three candles still alive and flickering from dinner. Her expression became soft and apologetic, and then she whispered *sorry* before snuffing it out with her fingers. Each candle received the same, loving treatment of being extinguished gently instead of

17

the harsh, sudden cutting off of its energy by blowing it out. I never tired of watching her do that.

"I hope this doesn't mean you're going to be bored all summer," she said, turning to me.

"Me, too," I said. The smell of spent candle curled through the room like a sad memory. For the briefest of moments I felt the loss, but quickly shook it off. I wasn't going to go there.

I tossed my keys on the counter and grabbed a glass for some water.

"So what *are* your plans for the summer?" my step-dad asked.

Shoving my glass under the ice dispenser of the fridge, I let a few cubes drop in. I paced my words, hoping to sound nonchalant. "I thought about asking Jesse to come up for a visit. Maybe I can convince him to stay awhile. Or…" I filled my glass with water, then turned to face him. "Maybe I could go down to L.A.?"

Since Jesse moved to Los Angeles, I'd been asking to visit him, but the answer was always the same. I was too young to be left unsupervised in Los Angeles. Jesse ran with a different crowd now. Being a mechanic in one of the top Porsche dealerships afforded him a lifestyle of the rich and famous. He had a lot of big name contacts and dated a lot of wealthy women – lonely wives would be my guess – and being as young as he was, he did a lot of clubbing and whatever good looking, well-off, twenty-one-year-olds did. Not the appropriate environment for a sixteen-year-old, as Mom would remind me. I knew it was a shot in the dark, but, hey, it was a shot worth taking.

"Maybe next summer," Mom said, planting a kiss to my cheek.

A shot that missed its target completely.

"Here's something to consider." Jon slid a brochure across the counter top and let it rest a good six inches from my hand. "Just think about it, okay?" As usual, not too intrusive, not too pushy, but still with continued encouragement.

"It's a retreat your mother and I are going on this weekend. Maybe you'd like to join us?" He spared me the effort of reading it. "Just three days, so it's not like you'd be locked in for very long."

Three days I could handle. Long enough for me to get a little space from the boredom of Sandpoint. On first glance, it actually looked interesting: *"Running with the Beast.* Three days of reconnecting with the gifts and energy of the Earth."* Just the name of it was enough to peak my interest.

Besides, getting away, if only for a little while, would help shift my focus away from Justin. I still had hope – hell, I'd always have hope – but until I figured out how to get inside his head, I had no choice but to wait.

# CHAPTER THREE

The drive through the Napa Valley in California was breathtaking. Rows and rows of grapevines stretched over the fields, like lifelines over the Earth's surface. We'd flown into Sacramento and drove the hundred miles to *Castello di Tranquillità*. I'd be lying if I said I wasn't excited about the retreat. There was nothing remotely like this in Illinois or near Sandpoint. The road leading to the castle was flanked by long rows of grapevines on one side and heavily forested land on the other.

"There, Jon," I pointed over his shoulder just to the left of the entrance sign. "I think that's where we're supposed to park. The brochure said they tried to 'hide the sight of the present from the feel of the past,'" I said, quoting what I'd read earlier.

"Spectacular, isn't it?" Jon looked out across the vineyards.

"Spectacular doesn't even begin to describe it," I said. "I can't wait to get started." I pulled out the brochure for the hundredth time to see the schedule.

Friday, the guests would learn to read tarot cards and palms. Saturday's schedule included *'Running with the Beast.'* According to the brochure, we'd be learning to see with our hearts, not our eyes, to find our way from one point to another. Seemed simple enough, though I had a feeling it would be anything but. There was no way the organizers of this retreat were going to invite a bunch of people to this amazing castle and make the activities simple. Sunday was set up for us to take everything we'd learned about the elements of water, fire, earth, and air, revisit each one, and put our thoughts to paper.

We grabbed our suitcases out of the car and headed up the stone pathway to the stairs leading to the castle entrance.

A small drawbridge had been lowered, spanning across the moat to give us access to the courtyard inside the walls. I felt a bit overdressed standing next to the sheep and goats that wandered around inside the walls. A burlap dress or something would have been more appropriate.

"I'll show you to your rooms." A member of the hosting party greeted us and gestured toward the doorway. Inside, the tapestries and medieval weapons on the walls created the ambiance of living in the sixteenth century. Even though the tapestries from different time periods softened the stone walls with their obvious richness, they didn't lessen the serious and hardened historic mood.

At the top of narrow stone steps, our host pushed on a wide door that opened into a small room. The wood stove in the corner and the two large beds pulled the walls closer together and kept tight company with each other.

"You'll have plenty of time to unpack your suitcases and rest," she smiled and pointed to the large dresser against one wall.

I eyed the wood stove tucked in the corner. That was one of the very few times I was grateful to have access to fire, because the chill that saturated the air clung to my body like a ghostly warning.

"The restrooms are down the hall on the right. Just past those are the private showers," our host announced. "Dinner will be served at 7:00 in the main hall," she added and then closed the door behind her.

"Wow. This is so cool." I put my suitcase on the floor next to one of the beds. Outside the window, other guests wandered on the lawn and the strip of dirt that edged the vines.

"I'm glad you decided to join us, Alyx." Mom crossed the room and wrapped her arms around me.

"I'm not making any promises, Mom," I said. I let her hug me a few seconds before pulling away. I agreed to come here because I was curious. Well, okay, more than curious.

Not only was hanging out in a castle all weekend too cool to pass up, but there was a tiny crack in my amour that had appeared a few years ago, and through that sliver of a window, the old me was trying to get out. And truth be told, I wanted to help her.

~ ~ ~

With tarot card and palm reading skills under my belt, I got up early Saturday morning, looking forward to the all-day schedule. I had no idea until after breakfast that it was going to be an all *night* session. Apparently I misread the brochure, thinking it said *a.m.* instead of *p.m.*, which had me thinking. What could we do that would last all night?

"This will be an interesting test for you, Alyx. For all of us," Mom said, during the short ride to the field where *Running with the Beast* would take place.

"Us" meant the dozen others we rode with on the retreat bus, looking like clones, wearing the same style of cotton pants, tunics, and robes.

Mom squeezed my hand.

"I wonder how long it'll take us to find the second fire," I said.

I was more than a little nervous. At first when they told us we would begin at one bonfire and the task was to find our way to another bonfire, I figured it couldn't be that difficult. But when they mentioned how big an area the playing field was, I hoped we had flashlights with some serious candlelight power. And why, of all symbols they could have used, did they choose bonfires at the start and finish? My excitement died the second they mentioned that part of the set up.

"Couldn't they have made the boundaries a little smaller? Why a five-mile radius? What if we go in the wrong direction?"

"It's actually a smaller area than most of these types of gatherings, but you'll find that the space will mean nothing when you can see with your other senses," Mom explained.

"That's just it," I said. "How will my other senses help me see in the dark?" I wasn't feeling so confident anymore.

Warmth spread through my hand when Mom placed hers over mine. "Just as a blind person's senses are heightened, yours will do the same tonight. It's all about trusting your instincts and becoming one with the elements – asking for their help and listening – *really* listening."

The brakes of the bus squeaked a little in protest when it stopped. The only indication that we had reached our destination was the glow of the small bonfire a short distance away. And as far as I could see, there wasn't another one within miles of us.

No one spoke much above a whisper as we shuffled single file off the bus into the waiting darkness, and pooled into a little group a few steps away. A minute or so later, a retreat member, flashlight in hand, stepped off a similar bus that had been following ours. Getting right back on the bus and going back to the castle suddenly seemed like a really good idea.

"Alyx," Jon said. "Don't even think about it."

I could hear the tease in his voice. "What? I wasn't—"

My mom's arm slipped around my waist. "You'll be fine, sweetie."

"Can we all go together? You know, have our own little pack?" I hated to be such a wimp.

She pulled me closer. "How can we hope to trust our own intuition if there are others around to overshadow it? The entire point of this is to let all expectations go and allow the elements to present themselves in a way only you can interpret."

Jon took hold of my hand and rubbed it between his own. Though the air around me was warm, my insides were shaking a little. In less than twenty minutes, I'd be on my own, in the dark, listening for who knows what, while trying to find another bonfire within the boundaries, which, I had a feeling, weren't marked very well. I probably would have made a break for it if Mom and Jon had not flanked me and led me toward the fire. I tried my last card: the guilt trip.

"How could you just leave me out here alone like this?"

"You won't really be alone," she said.

"What if something happens to me out there?"

She squeezed my hand. "I believe in you, Alyx." I've told you before - you're unique and very gifted. Your energy will draw the help you need. I'm not worried about you at all."

So much for the guilt. Her confidence in me is what was tripping me up. What if I messed this up? What if the house fire in Illinois was because I didn't have the skills I was supposed to have?

"Can I have everyone's attention?" The retreat leader stood in front of us and waited until everyone focused on her.

"The beginning point is at this bonfire. Notice that it is enclosed with black rocks. The finishing bonfire is somewhere within the boundaries of a five-mile radius. That fire is enclosed with white rocks. This is the opportunity to open your mind and heart and receive the love and gifts the Earth elements generously offer. Trust yourselves. Put your ego aside for the night and believe that you will be guided to the location of the second fire." She paused and looked at each of us. "You will be sightless, but be assured the elements will speak to you if you listen. The wind will nudge you, water will talk to your heart, fire will light your way, and the earth will be your foundation. Once you open yourself to these elements, they will forever stay with you, should you allow them to."

She paused and looked around the group. "Are there any questions?"

The crackling flames popped impatiently as if trying to quiet the murmurs of the participants.

"Then we shall begin," she said.

The gathering broke apart and everyone drifted into different directions.

Mom hugged me tight and whispered, "I'm so proud of you, baby. Do your best. I'll see you at the other fire."

"Okay, but please come looking for me if I don't show up."

"I'd never leave you." She grasped my hand one more time and then turned to Jon. They hugged and walked away, leaving me alone. In the dark. Without a freakin' clue.

# CHAPTER FOUR

The stillness in the air amplified my breathing. With my back to the fire, I waited until my eyes adjusted to the darkness that closed in on me. Shuffling feet on my left and eerie silence on my right had me off balance. I couldn't see my shoes. I couldn't see my hands. I couldn't see the sky. Closing my eyes didn't shed any more light on a solution either, but I hoped the other senses would kick in to make up for my loss of sight.

I had to do something. Standing in one spot wasn't going to get me to the other fire. The elements would guide me – or so they told me. Of the four - air, water, fire, earth - earth was the one element that didn't change. It was what we build upon. It was reliable. And it was as all I had.

I slipped off my shoes and centered my weight. Squeezing my eyes tight, I visualized my feet growing roots and passing through the grass and dirt, then wrapping around the rocks below. My worries passed through to the waiting ground and were replaced with the stability and endurance of the Earth. The cool air slipped past my lips into my lungs effortlessly and without a sound. Gravity pulled my shoulders down, causing me to stand taller and with confidence.

It might have been a minute or two that had passed, or maybe ten or twenty. Nothing had changed. No bonfire magically appeared. No lights. No guide showing the way. *Damn.* I knew stuff like that didn't just happen, that it takes time to get on the right vibe, but time wasn't something I had much of. I put my shoes on and started walking. It wasn't long before I started questioning if I was going in the right direction. I hadn't seen any fires or any of the other group members. Aside from a fence that took forever to find a way around, the space around me was empty.

Uncertainty has a way of freezing those parts of us that keep us moving forward – in this case, my feet. They stopped mid-stride, waiting for a signal from my mind to move ahead.

I spun around, suddenly disoriented. So much darkness suffocated me, squeezing the air from my lungs from the inside out. Inky black coated my skin, seeped into my mouth, and claimed my eyes and ears. The abyss. It was exactly like it had been six years ago when my common sense completely froze and sent me headlong into a blind panic. That hysteria began the domino effect and ultimate demise of the life I knew - the life that I both loved and hated. My fists tightened with resolve until they ached. I *was* going to make this happen. I *would* make it to the other fire.

But I needed help.

"Hello?" I called out to the night hoping for another human voice. Muffled silence wrapped around me, like a velvet-lined box, making me feel that I was enclosed in a container, rather than standing in the harsh, unfiltered expanse of night. I kicked off my shoes again, stood firm, and dug my toes into the damp dirt, focused entirely on establishing a connection. Tingling filtered up through the bottom of my feet and stoked my confidence a little, but not enough.

"Help me," I whispered, tilting my chin and blinking into the night sky, waiting… and waiting.

The sound of rushing water rose up and crushed the silence, like an underground spring breaking the surface and gasping for air.

"What the hell?" I spun in the direction of the sound. "Where did you come from?" I grabbed my shoes and ran in the direction of what sounded like a river - a river that couldn't have been there before. It was possible that I was so focused on hearing other sounds that I had been oblivious to this one, but… no. That noise would be hard to ignore.

When Mom had been part of a coven, she'd done gatherings similar to this. She told me about fences that she ran into, huge holes in the ground, clusters of thorn bushes that appeared in her path that, when she went back days later, weren't there. Those were things that most would consider unbelievable, but to the coven, they were signs and blessings.

So which one was the river? Something to guide me, or to challenge me? Or was this free-flowing river merely something for me to discover the meaning of?

When I got to its edge, I didn't know how to interpret this. Upstream, downstream, or straight across. Hell, maybe it was symbolic of my life. Crouching along the side, I jabbed my fingers in the chilly water to test for depth. There was no way to know how fast the water was going, how deep or how wide it was. I supposed I could follow it, a little like a yellow brick road, but was *that* the right choice?

The stars were all-knowing and all-seeing. I mean, they're up there, watching everything that goes on down here right?

"Come on," I whispered to them. "A clue."

Delivery was quick. I spun around at the one sound I really, really didn't want to hear. My hands were thrust out in front of me, waving them in a threatening way, but I had no idea what I was waving at.

A low-pitched growl came from the left. I spun and shielded myself against a slight movement of space to my right.

*Shit!* The air in my lungs was caught in my chest and I couldn't work up the scream that sat behind it. Something brushed the back of my legs, almost making them buckle. I spun around again. There was no way I was going to down without a fight. Closing my eyes cut out the distraction of the things I *thought* were out there and I focused instead on the shifting air for any movement. There was an unrest, mirrored in the tiny whimper that carried on the breeze.

Adrenaline found its way into my bloodstream and filled my leg muscles. I turned to the sweet, clear, lyrical song of the rushing water, hoping like hell these dogs or wolves weren't going to jump on my back.

Landing in thigh-deep water sent an instant numbing shock through my body and stiffened my joints. The water dropped to my shins, then my ankles as I splashed across. My toe caught on a rock and sent me sprawling on the other side, but I got up and kept running, keeping my ears open and my palms out, every so often stopping and listening for any sound besides the thudding of my heart. But there was nothing to guide me, nothing to force me to make a decision.

I slowed my pace. The ache in my chest eased up and my breaths found a steady pattern. From the looks of the lightening sky, I'd been wandering around for, what, seven hours, maybe? Where did the night go?

"Alyx." My voice was loud in the predawn silence. "You're up the creek without a bonfire." The stars were probably having a great laugh at me. "Yeah, yeah, yeah," I said, looking to the sky.

Heading up a gentle slope, motivation and energy drained out my soles and left an imprint in the grass beneath my steps. I closed my eyes and again asked for help. What I *really* wanted was the bus to take me back to the castle, but I'd settle for a safe place to lie down.

Letting my lids take their time to open, I took in the most welcome, breathtaking sight, one I swore I'd never forget. A large willow tree, its branches silhouetted against the pre-dawn light, that broadened as I walked closer. The drooping branches dipped over me like an umbrella and seemed to point to a clearing at the base of the trunk.

My safe place.

Sinking down into the dirt, I pulled my legs close to my chest and pressed my forehead against my knees. I thought I could do this. I wanted to beat this and prove to Mom I had learned, that I had matured. I wanted to know if I had the connection and insight. Tipping my head back, I closed my eyes against the stars that blinked with fading strength through the branches and leaves of the willow.

*Please let them find me soon.*

The familiar hum of energy connected with my feet and my toes responded by digging deep into the earth, releasing the sweet smell of the fertile soil into the growing dawn.

There will be another time. Another chance to prove myself, as long as my mom had faith in me. Right now, though, I was too tired to care.

# CHAPTER FIVE

Taylor snapped her phone shut and reached for her jacket. "We're going to the old shack with Jake and everybody."

She hadn't been at my house for more than ten minutes before she'd texted around and started making plans. I stayed focused on the magazine I'd been flipping through so she wouldn't see my eyes roll. Whenever we hooked up with "everybody," Jake and Todd in particular, things usually got a little whacked out. Like when they picked a fight with a tourist at the bowling alley, for no apparent reason, and got us kicked out. Or the time they pulled the "fire-in-the-hole" prank at one of the fast-food restaurants. Todd and Jake thought it was hilarious when Jake ordered a soft drink and tossed it back at the girl in the window. The cop sitting in his car in the parking lot didn't think it was all that funny.

I really didn't want to go to the shack. I wanted to stay home and maybe watch a movie. Besides, the shack was in a creepy area of Sandpoint, where people lived off the grid and stayed out of sight. I don't think anyone had lived in the shack for years, so a lot of kids went there to party. I wasn't into it.

"So what if I don't want to go?" I asked.

In one quick motion, Taylor grabbed the magazine from my lap and yanked on my wrist hard enough to pull me to my feet.

"Come on. This will be fun. We haven't been to the shack for a long time."

Tugging on my wrist, I pointed out, "We haven't just hung out and watched a movie for a long time, either."

Her foot came down in a petulant stomp. Right on cue.

"Come on," she said again. "I don't want to go without you. Besides, Caleb will be there."

Caleb. Her plaything of the month. Pure filler material. This time I let her see my eyes roll.

"It's kind of cold tonight," I said, twisting my wrist out of her grip.

"It's not that cold. Besides, we'll have a bonfire."

My breath hitched before I could stop it. I turned and pretended to cough. It didn't do much to ease the anxiety, but I hoped it was enough to distract Taylor. Knowing Jake and Todd, the fire would be bigger than I'd be comfortable with.

"I think I'll pass," I said.

Taylor held the magazine just out of my grasp when I reached for it.

"Look at me, Alyx," she said, maneuvering her face in front of mine. "You had a funny look when I mentioned the bonfire." Her eyes narrowed. "Are you afraid?"

Instead of turning away, I should have faced her and my stupid fear head on. But I didn't. Sometimes I underestimate her perception.

Again, she moved in front of me and pointed a finger in my face. "You *are* afraid, aren't you?"

I bit my lip to keep it from trembling. Of course fire scared the crap out of me, but I refused to let her see how much.

"What happened? Did you get burned or something when you were little?"

Compassion was never one of Taylor's strong points, so when I didn't answer, she changed tactics. "It's only a small, itty, bitty fire. There's no way it'll get out of control."

Oh, she had no idea…

"Whatever happened to you, it couldn't have been that bad." She planted her hands on her hips.

Things would have gotten very uncomfortable between us had I not shoved six years' worth of fear and anger into my fists and locked them in tight. The emotions fell from my face and a practiced smile slid into position.

"It's not the fire, Taylor. It's Jake and Todd I don't like. They're so freakin' annoying." I smoothed over the lie with the truth.

She considered this for a few moments, then her eyes lost their accusing squint.

"Well, if that's all, it's no big deal," she shrugged. "Just ignore them. You're going to be with me."

~ ~ ~

Out of the nine of us there, I was the odd one out. Megan and Crystal were hooked up with Scott and Andrew, Taylor was with Caleb, and Jake and Todd sat with a six pack of beer between them. I sat away from everyone – not with Taylor like she said I would. Honestly, though, I was glad. Taylor probably would have insisted we sit closer to the fire to keep the chill off. I was perfectly fine where I was – ten feet away, just beyond the unseen wall where I should be able to feel the heat.

The unmistakable sound of deep inhalation followed by silence made me cringe. Dumb and Dumber were getting wasted *and* stoned. The smell of weed crept over and invaded my space. I wished I stayed home.

I covered my nose and avoided looking into the fire. I focused instead on the red embers burning the end of my cigarette. Still hot, still born from a flame, but not as intimidating as what danced in front of me. I took up smoking a couple years ago, but it was my way of having control of my fear of fires. Each time I lit up was a small victory for me. I almost had the beast beaten. Even though fire still scared me, I wasn't running away. It was all about baby steps.

The stench of skunk weed pushed against my face when Todd squatted next to me. He offered me his joint.

I shook my head. "No thanks. I don't smoke pot."

"Oh, like that's better for you?" He pointed to my cigarette.

"At least this doesn't make me stupid," I shot back.

"Bitch," he muttered. He stood up and walked to the other side of the fire where Caleb and Taylor were tangled in a lip lock.

Huh. Well, Todd's comment certainly didn't help my mood. Neither did watching Caleb and Taylor making out. It was so easy for her to go from guy to guy. I never understood how someone did that. Then again, I've never had a lot of boyfriends like Taylor had. I was old fashioned, I guess. My body and my heart couldn't be separated from my emotions.

A deep, grumbling burp broke the relative quiet.

"Oh, God, Jake! Don't be so gross!" Megan punched him in the shoulder.

He laughed. "You ain't seen nothin'!"

His beer can hit the rocks that circled the bonfire before bouncing in. Perfect. The tipping point from stupid to asinine.

And right on cue, *whoots* and girlie screams egged him on to reach his personal best for the highest pee arch.

"I'm sorry," I whispered to the fire. "That's just so wrong."

"Hey! Check it out." Todd faced the dark space behind us. "A zombie dog."

We looked to where he pointed. Just outside the glow of the bonfire stood a dog with short, kind of mangy, tan-colored fur.

"Eww." Megan cringed. "He's missing an eye."

I stood up and stepped closer to the dog. A scar slashed deep across its right eye, making it only look as if his eye was missing. But his right front leg definitely was.

"Come here, boy," Todd said, patting his thigh in encouragement.

"Todd, don't," I said. "Leave him alone."

36

He shot me a *yeah, right* look and started after the dog, who hopped back a little, but wasn't fast enough to escape Todd's reach.

Todd picked up the dog, turned, and started toward the fire.

"Put him down," I demanded, putting myself in front of him.

Todd was a good six inches taller than me and outweighed me by at least fifty pounds. His grip on the dog tightened every time it twisted around to try to bite him. Todd was so high, I doubted he would know if he'd gotten bit anyway.

He snorted and pushed past me like I was nothing.

"Zombie dogs have to be destroyed," Todd said in a voice I'm sure was meant to mimic some obnoxious zombie movie he'd seen. He succeeded in sounding stupid and only pissed me off.

Helpless in Todd's hold, the dog spread its paws out in front of him as they got closer to the heat. Its body wiggled and twisted to break free. It didn't matter if Todd was serious or not because the dog's panic became mine. Its haggard breaths echoed my own and its wide eyes glistened with growing fear of the unknown.

My pulse raced, threatening to explode out of my jugular.

"Damn it, Todd! Stop it! You're scaring him!" I grabbed his arm.

Totally stoned from the weed, he stopped and looked down at me, eyes glazed over as if he'd forgotten that I was there.

Across the fire Taylor and Caleb had stopped making out and stared, mouths hanging open. The others looked equally shocked, but outside of shaking their heads or whispering to each other, none of them made a move.

"Would one of you freakin' help?" My voice was rough against my dry throat.

The glassy look in Todd's eyes cleared and he easily shook me off.

I lunged at him again, this time taking his collar in both hands and yanking back with all my weight.

He lost his balance and caught his heel on a rock, landing hard on his back.

"Oww!"

The dog wiggled free as soon as Todd hit the ground and used his chest to gain traction.

"Goddamn dog! What the hell, Alyx?"

"No, what the *hell*, Todd? What were you thinking?" It didn't matter what his answer was because I didn't care. He didn't get it. None of them did. They couldn't feel the flames startle in response to the beer cans or Jake's brilliant arc of pee. Even though the trees were still, their whispered discord sifted through the leaves. The earth felt it. I felt it.

I don't know. Maybe it was me who didn't understand.

~ ~ ~

I finally came to a conclusion. It doesn't matter what face we show the world. If it's not who we really are, our true, authentic self will eventually break through. It may take awhile, but it'll happen.

The reflection in my mirror was beginning to look less like me and more like my mother. My eyes had lost the superficial animation and emanated their own glow; the blue was bluer and the shine was brighter.

What held me back all those years was that, even though I knew I was a light worker, I saw what my mother went through. The spiritual, mystical, healing arts woman that she was actually scared people. They marked her as "woo-woo." I won't lie. After moving to Sandpoint, I worried about what the others would say about me if they found out I practiced with Mom. I wanted to forget everything she taught me, every spell and ritual she showed me. But deep down I knew it'd be impossible to deny it. By chasing after a life that was never mine, I thought I could run from what I was destined to live – a path I was meant to follow.

I plopped down on my bed.

"What am I doing?" I whispered.

I shuffled the oracle cards, but nothing felt right. The cards weren't talking to me. I had questions and I wanted answers, or rather confirmation of what I already knew. After dealing with everyone's stupidity at the shack, I needed a road map to take me far away from them.

Placing the cards back in their pouch and grabbing the nail polish from my night stand, I settled back against the headboard. I was ready for a change.

Short strokes of the brush coated my fingernails with inky black color. For some, black meant darkness, depression, absence of light. For me, it represented shadows and invisibility. It meant space, as in the universe, space that needed to be filled.

It was time to put away the rainbows and get serious.

# CHAPTER SIX

"Are you sure you want to do this?" Mom asked, her brows arching a little.

"Definitely," I said. "Besides, it's a little late now."

She looked from me to the bank lady then back to me. Her chest rose and fell with a resolute sigh.

"Okay." She picked up the pen and scribbled her signature along the bottom of the page next to mine, signing ownership of my Audi over to the new owner.

The loan manager smiled and, scooping up the paperwork, promised to return with my check.

The intensity of Mom's stare was too much to ignore. It seemed like she was looking for an opening into my thoughts. I raised my brows in a silent *what?* and returned her gaze.

She brushed my overgrown bangs off my face. "So now what?" she asked. "Would you like a ride somewhere?"

"No, it's okay. It'll be good to walk around for a while."

"Are you ever going to tell me why the sudden change?"

My shoulders lifted and dropped, something I seemed to be doing a lot of lately.

"I want my friends to like me, not the stuff that I have." I looked at the only person I knew who was completely certain of herself, entirely comfortable with her abilities, and would never let anyone sway her. Yeah, I still wanted to be strong like her. "Maybe it's your pagan influence that's finally sinking in."

One brow lifted very, very slightly. "You know money doesn't define our beliefs or spirituality."

I nodded. We were tree-hugging, Earth-loving, high-vibrating people who drove nice cars and lived on the lake. I knew it didn't mean we weren't in touch with the elements.

But I used the parties, the clothes, and the cars as a cover to hide behind, and that shield was becoming threadbare in some places.

Selling my Audi served two purposes: to see if the person my friends saw was good enough without it, and, probably more important, whether the face I saw every morning in the mirror was good enough without it.

"It's all right, Mom." I grasped her hand and squeezed, hoping to reassure her. "I'm going to my bank and then check out a couple cars I saw in the paper. I'll call you when I need a ride home."

Mom took in a large, slow breath as if filling her lungs with words she wanted to say, then let it out slowly, leaving the words unspoken. "Okay." She smiled and her face relaxed. "Just let me know where you are."

I started to tell her not to worry when the bank lady returned and sat behind her desk. She stapled the papers together, and handed me my own set of documents with a check clipped to the top. "You're all set."

And for the first time in a long while, I believed I was.

# CHAPTER SEVEN

Under the florescent lights in my bathroom, the blue of my irises and the blonde wisps of hair that fell around my face screamed California girl, but I hadn't been feeling so sunshiny the last few days. I ran my fingers through my hair. This would be the last time the strands would be coated with blonde. I squeezed them in my fists and let my decision sink in. I was going to be me, and only me. I wasn't exactly certain where that might lead, but strength and conviction had found its way up to the surface.

Conflicting emotions of not wanting to let go and wanting to move forward slammed against each other before melting together into a quiet acceptance. Still, the underlying disappointment of what I had become was overwhelmingly obvious in my face. I had ignored me for so long, but found it was easier to cry behind a mask than to explain what the problem is. I couldn't tell Taylor, or anyone else, how I felt about my dad, about moving here, about wanting to learn the craft like my mom, and how much I missed listening to the rhythm of the Earth. They'd think I was nuts. Well, I was over that. I was about to make myself a huge target for them to ridicule if they needed to. I had no problem with that.

"All right. Let's do this," I said to my reflection before I could change my mind. "Black hair it is."

In just over an hour, my hair was cut, colored, and blown dry. It wasn't a great cut by a long shot, but years of my veil now lay in the trash, ready to be tossed out with the cotton balls and wadded-up Kleenex. I drew a thick line of black to harness the blue of my eyes, and black lipstick pulled my new look together.

Every change I made was exciting, but not without a twinge of guilt. I had such an easy time letting go of the past, erasing the last six years of my life, but this time I wasn't running from anything. I was ready to face my past head-on, ready to take it down if it tried to consume me again.

Scooping a handful of clothes off the floor, I threw them into the hamper on my way to the closet. I flipped through dozens of colorful shirts that hung on the rack, and opted for the loosest-fitting black shirt I had. In the back of the closet I found a stash of clothes that I rarely wore – black jeans and black ankle boots. Those were gifts from Aunt Sarah that I had dismissed as too serious to wear. Now they seemed entirely appropriate. I grabbed a beanie on my way out and covered all but just a few strands of the new me.

Black, the epitome of invisibility. After the last few years of being so colorful and loud, I needed some downtime. Today I was going for the stealth look.

~ ~ ~

Though selling my car was the right choice for me, unveiling the Audi's replacement officially to my friends was an entirely different matter.

The ad claimed the car to be "gently used" but I wouldn't have described it that way. When I first brought my little black Subaru home, it looked like it had been around the block more than a few times. The engine needed some work, but Jesse was going to fly up from Los Angeles to fix that.

The afternoon was going to be a game changer. Between the car and my new choice of fashion, I was asking my friends to accept a lot all at once.

I anticipated Taylor's judgments, but then again, maybe *I* was being too quick to judge. Maybe it wouldn't matter to Taylor. I hoped not, but honestly, her attitude was beginning to annoy me. She behaved as if her family's middle class status placed her above everyone. I could only imagine what she'd say about me now.

~ ~ ~

I wasn't surprised that Taylor didn't rush out of her house when I pulled up to the curb. The living room curtains shifted a little as someone looked out at the street, but the front door never opened.

*I'm outside,* I texted her.

She came rushing out a minute later, but stopped, looking a bit confused, then scowled when Megan and Crystal ran into the back of her.

I gave her a few seconds to look up and down the street for my Audi then let her off the hook by tapping on the horn.

"Well, that's impressive," I said, shaking my head. The small, pathetic-sounding squeak that slipped out from underneath my hood was embarrassing, but well worth the look on Taylor's face.

The front passenger side window groaned all the way down. When I waved her over, her jaw went slack. It was a priceless moment to see her caught off guard.

She closed the distance between her house and my car and leaned over to get a better look. Her gaze shuffled between me and the inside of the car, her eyes growing wider every second.

Megan's hand did a lousy job of covering her smirk.

Taylor stood straight, looked at the others, then stuck her head inside the window again.

"Alyx? What the hell? Is there a theme party at Skate Plaza I don't know about?"

"Are you getting in or not?" I asked, blatantly ignoring her question.

Megan and Crystal climbed in the back seat without any hesitation, but Taylor blinked, as if clicking through her options. She finally let out a long, low sigh, yanked the door open, and got into the front seat.

She pushed her hair off her face she said, "So. What happened to your car? When do you get it back?"

"I don't. I sold it," I said.

"Did your parents make you sell it?" Megan asked.

Taylor's eye widened. "Oh, my God! *What* did you *do*?"

I couldn't imagine what she was thinking. Mom and I have never had any kind of disagreement, let alone me doing something horrible enough to justify selling my car.

The seconds passed, leaning on the question that hung between us.

I finally shrugged. "Nothing. It was my choice."

Taylor's brows shot up. "*Excuse* me? You traded in your Audi for…" She seemed to be trying to choose her words carefully. "… this? *Why*?"

Her incredulousness was such a joke. This all coming from a person who had no car, who depended on others for her transportation. You'd think she'd be grateful for any set of wheels. I'd definitely been spoiling her.

"Oh, it's not that bad, Taylor," Crystal came to my rescue.

We exchanged looks in the rear view mirror. "Thanks, Crys."

"But why?" Taylor asked again.

"Because it was time for a change."

"You should paint it, Alyx," Megan said. "You know, like white or something. Black is so… black."

Taylor leaned into the seat, her back barely touching the fabric. Her internal *eww* radar oozed from the lines of her frown.

"There's nothing wrong with the car, Taylor," I said. "The carpets and seats were cleaned yesterday. And look," I pointed to the fragrance tree that hung from the stereo knob. "Strawberry."

She tilted her head back and sniffed. "I guess it's okay. And your clothes do match the color of your car... but your hair, too?" Taylor's lips pressed into a tight line, probably to stop from saying anything more.

I pulled my beanie down a little farther over my ears. "Yeah. My hair, too."

I tried to catch Crystal's eye in the rear view mirror, but she looked away. Megan stayed quiet, too. This was going to be a long ride, and I wasn't just talking about the trip to Coeur d'Alene.

# CHAPTER EIGHT

"So what's up with you? Why are you dressing so… Emo?"

I looked down at my bare feet dangling over the water at City Beach, the wood planks of the dock warm under my thighs.

The weather hadn't heated up yet, but the sun drew the locals outside their homes and on their bikes and in their boats. The beach, though, was empty except for a few kids who didn't mind the freezing water.

Taylor leaned over and grabbed hold of my feet. "You're Emo down to your toenails."

I peered at her from underneath my bangs. "I'm not Emo," I said, pulling my feet back. "Just because I'm wearing black nail polish doesn't mean I have repressed anger or anything."

"Then what *are* you?" Her eyes squinted ever so slightly and her mouth curled in a hint of a sneer.

Good question. Well, I was mostly in the dark and still discovering who I was. I waited six years to wake up from what I had hoped was a bad dream. And now, with this metamorphosis underway, I had only one answer:

"I'm me." I buried her stare with my own. "I'm just me."

Taylor's brows squished together as if she was expecting another response, something not quite so simple.

"But everything about you has changed. I mean, your car, your clothes, your hair…" she said, leaning in to grab the ends of my midnight-black hair.

"Does it bother you?" I asked.

"No." she said, letting the strands slip between her fingers.

I expected some resistance and had even been prepared for the same treatment Mom got back in Illinois. So I pushed her further.

"Do you still want to hang out with me, clothes and all?" From behind my cheap sunglasses, my gaze challenged her, grateful she couldn't see the disappointment to the answer I knew would come.

"Well, yeah." Instead of looking at me, she focused on a passing boat. "Of course I do."

Heh. It's amazing how those four little words – *of course I do* – could be so telling. I didn't believe any one of them.

~ ~ ~

I didn't hear much from Taylor after that day at the dock. Her excuses to avoid me were creative, and I supposed plausible, but it boiled down to the one truth: she wanted to keep her distance. Which was fine with me. I didn't have much room for the superficial bullshit and the knee-deep drama that followed her, anyway.

At the same time, though, I was going to miss the others because, with the exit of Taylor, the rest of the group followed. The friend list of a misfit, misunderstood, dark Alyx, took a nosedive.

I had the rest of the summer to get used to my unpopular status. I would have the next month to seriously learn from Mom again. It also freed me up to spend time with Jesse without Taylor or the others fawning all over him.

As a brother, Jesse was awesome. Always was – even though the house fire ordeal put us on shaky ground for a while.

I really missed him since he moved away. There was a time when my dad's attitude isolated us from everyone. Making friends became too painful when Dad would find one thing after another wrong with them and they'd finally stayed away. Dad even tried to isolate Jesse from Mom and me, saying stuff like, "He's a man's man. I won't have him doin' any of that voodoo crap you women do." Even after we stopped doing that "voodoo crap" when Dad was around, Jesse kept his distance to keep the peace. But I knew with every wink, every mischievous smile, Jesse was still on my side.

Looking at him across the engine of my car, I could see why he was so successful in L.A. Though he never pursued the Craft, he still had the gift of intuitive touch. He could sense energy with his hands. That was one of the reasons he was so good at fixing cars, and why he was so popular with the women. More important than his California-tanned, gym-toned body, sun-streaked brown hair, and boyish smile, he knew how to make people feel good about themselves.

Peeling off his grease-stained latex gloves, he gave me one of his winning smiles that showed off his adorable dimples. "Well, I can't do much about the outside, but the inside purrs like a kitten now."

"This is so awesome, Jesse. Thank you, thank you, thank you!" I skirted around the front of the car and met him halfway. He wrapped his arms around me and gave me a big-brother hug, lifting me off my feet. The moment my feet touched the ground, he pulled back and leveled his face with mine.

"Hey, are you okay?" he asked, his dimples quickly disappearing.

"Yeah, why?"

"I don't know." He shrugged. "Just this sudden change." His sweeping hand indicated everything about me. "I mean, don't get me wrong. I like it. But from an Audi to an old Subaru… the make-up and clothes."

"Hey," I held my hands up to block the words from permeating the space between us. "No dissin' the car. And the clothes… well, they're just more my style."

"Is this what your friends are wearing, too? Like Taylor?"

I shook my head, toeing the garage floor with my shoe. "Nope. Only me. This isn't *her* style." I didn't let him see my eye-roll because I didn't want him to think I was being bitchy about it. Which I was. Totally. I thought I knew Taylor so well. I thought that she'd accept me for who I was no matter what. It wasn't the first time I was wrong about someone. "Besides, she's not really my friend anymore."

"Really?" Jesse scooped me up again and hugged me tight. "Well, I think you look great and that you're the most amazing girl. Taylor doesn't know what she's giving up."

This time I held onto him a little longer and a little tighter than I normally would, soaking up the acceptance.

He let me down again and kissed my forehead. "So, little sister. Aren't you curious to hear what this motor sounds like now?" he said, jerking his head in the direction of my car.

As if I needed a reminder.

I knew without a doubt, he had done his magic on my engine. I couldn't stop a smile from dominating my face. I ran to the driver's side, threw open the door, and slid behind the wheel. Turning the key was like slicing through butter, and the motor turned over without a sound.

Jesse eased down the hood and gently pressed on it until it clicked shut. Our eyes locked through the windshield. I couldn't tell which one of us had the bigger smile.

# CHAPTER NINE

Sinking deeper in the seat and pushing my sunglasses snug against my face completed the invisibility factor for me. I'd gone into hiding until I completely split open the skin of my old self and peeled it away to let the raw, new skin heal.

I drove down Oak Street, looking for a particular garage sale. I'd already scored some cool stuff earlier in the day – leggings, jackets, and scarves – all in my new favorite color of black. The clothes were more worn in and comfortable than the clothes I bought online. The prize find for the day was a camo backpack. I wasn't sure what I would use it for, but it was such a steal, I couldn't resist. Ha! Miss Popular turned Dark, toting around a camo backpack. Only in Idaho.

I double checked the ad I circled in the newspaper. It said it was an estate sale. Apart from the creepiness of picking through a dead person's belongings, you could usually find some cool and unusual things.

Cars prowled the overcrowded street, the drivers rubber-necking as they eyed the layout of the yard. There was so much stuff. The owner probably never threw anything away.

I pulled my car into a spot just as another car left, and turned the motor off.

"Sorry," I said to my car, patting the dashboard. "One last stop."

Tables had been placed on the driveway and in the garage. The first table had all sorts of shoes on it. I needed a couple more pairs of flats, which was exactly what the owner had a lot of. The shoes were a half size bigger than I wore, but I'd make it work.

The table next to the shoes was weighed down with books. Lots of old books. My kind of books. Judging from the collection, the former lady of the house was up there in age. Scattered among the stacks of literary classics were books protected by fabric covers. I counted 18 of them, the titles covering subjects of numerology, tarot, occult, metaphysics, and magic. Notes in small, meticulous handwriting crowded the margins of the pages. Phrases that meant something to the reader were underscored. Over half the books were reprints of work published in the mid-1930s. Some things in this universe were timeless.

One book in particular was far more commanding than the others. It was big and heavy. The print on the ornate cover was in a heavy script, so it was difficult to read, but I was able to make out the last line. *Ancient Mysteries and Secret Societies.*

The book was typeset in small print, as if someone wanted to shove hundreds of years' worth of Earth-old knowledge within the covers. Spread across the pages of proper English were passages describing Atlantis, sorcery, hidden magic, rituals, symbols and drawings, and old hieroglyphic-type images dotted each page.

My breath caught and fierce tingling ran the length of my spine, burst outward to my arms and neck, and out through my fingers. Something about this book was either very right or very wrong.

Across the yard a young woman was taking cash from another customer. I waved her over.

"Wow!" the woman said, when she got to my side. "Looks like you and my grandmother have something in common."

"She has a great collection." I said, being sure to keep my voice low. "Two dollars each, right?" I couldn't believe they were dumping them for that price.

She nodded.

"Here you go," I said, handing her two twenty-dollar bills. "Can you lend me a hand with these?" I asked. I couldn't wait to take a closer. This was such an amazing find, my entire body still buzzed. Mom was going to flip out. I looked around the yard one more time. As far as I was concerned, I needed nothing more.

# CHAPTER TEN

"Fire is your element, Alyx." Mom carefully set up a candle on the floor between us. "You'll learn to harness its energy easier than you will the other energies. We'll tap into it a little today."

Pouring over my new books had me fired up and ready to get on with the next step, and Mom was more than happy to start teaching me again. As I sat across from her, though, with matches and a candle between us, the memories of Illinois crushed any sense of curiosity and willingness to open up. I was about to face my demon in every sense of the word – and I wasn't looking forward to it. Not anymore.

Mom pulled a match from the box and slid it shut. She paused with the tip poised over the striking surface and raised her brows.

"Ready?"

I nodded, "As ready as I'll ever be, I guess." But even as I said the words, I doubted them. I had enough trouble keeping away the visions of our house burning down without the added fear of having the same situation reenacted in my room. Mom thought it would help with the healing process. I wasn't so sure about that.

She lit the candle.

My breath and pulse quickened as fast as it did six years ago when I did the same ceremony in my room in Illinois, without the slightest idea of what I was doing. All I knew then was that I wanted my parents not to fight.

It was the same ritual I saw my mom do so many times after they fought. I thought if I did it right, if I said the words to make the flame rise like Mom did, that when Dad came home, everything would be fine. I'd been so careful. Putting the candle on the windowsill seemed like a good idea at the time. And it would have been – had the flame stood still instead of thrashing around, had I been able to control it, had it not expanded the way it did, had the tip not touched the curtains…

"Alyx." A crease in her brow marred Mom's usually calm features.

I couldn't tell if she was angry or concerned. Was she thinking about that night, too? I'd sworn to her that it wasn't intentional, that I was just trying to help. If only they hadn't fought so much. If only Dad had stayed away instead of passing out in the den that night. If only he'd driven home instead of walking, then we would have seen his car. But we had no idea he was inside the house. We had escaped, leaving him in the den to die.

"Alyx, come back to me."

I dragged my gaze from the candle and followed her comforting voice to where the light reflected in her eyes.

"It'll be okay. You can do this," she said.

The candle flickered its challenge.

"Yeah." I wiped my sweaty palms over my skirt. "I can do this." The small fire extinguisher next to me was my safety net.

Mom reached over and squeezed my hand before holding her palm next to mine. Almost instantaneously a stream of heat connected the center of our palms and bound them together. My fingers curled in response and our hands caged a palpable ball of energy.

The flame between our hands crackled and expanded, but I didn't back down. I found strength in the force that we held in our palms.

"I'm going to move my fingers over the wick. Let's keep the ball's shape… like this."

Mom rotated her hand over the unwavering tentacle of fire. The tip dipped under each finger, popping up in between, as she slowly turned her wrist. I was afraid to breathe as she repeated the movement the other way, until our hands returned to their original position.

"Your turn," she said quietly.

"I can do this," I said again. I didn't know who I was trying to convince.

"You don't believe you can, do you?"

"Of course I do," I said, my eyes never leaving the flame. *Of course I do.* Those words again. "I can do this," I whispered. I started the motion of turning my hand and had every intention of going through with it, but when the skin on my pinky finger went from warm to hot, I backed off.

Mom moved her hand with mine, keeping the energy ball firmly between us, making it impossible to break the bond.

"It's a matter of getting on the same frequency as the element you are trying to manipulate or become one with," she said. "Each element has its own vibration. If you aren't connecting on the same level, then, in this case, the fire will scorch you. You need true intent and commitment." She waited until she was certain I was listening. "Trust that the fire will not burn you. That knowledge is inside you already, Alyx. Reach for it."

The space behind my right eye pulsed a few beats, sort of like someone tapping on my brain, telling me to focus. There was a presence, or awareness, pushing me from under and behind, swelling up like a wave. I shook it off. If I didn't have the confidence to back it up, this whole experience would be a total failure and I would definitely get burned.

"Keep trying." Mom said.

"There's a conflict somewhere in here." I pulled my hand away, breaking the connection with Mom. I tapped a finger to my forehead. "Something in here is pushing me to keep going, but I'm definitely fighting it." I filled my lungs with as much air as they would hold and then let it out. "I need to get through these blocks before I do this again."

She bit her lip and held her gaze to mine. Then said, "Of course. I wouldn't want it any other way."

We gathered the candle and matches and placed them in a basket. She leaned over and kissed my forehead and without a word, picked everything up and left me to figure this out on my own.

# CHAPTER ELEVEN

"May I help you find something?"

My first step inside Inquire Within bookstore was undeniably comfortable. Maybe "familiar" would better describe it. Books lined the wall to my left. Candles and incense to my right infused the air with their sweet and spicy fragrances. In the back of the store a handful of people had their chairs in a circle, where a book discussion was being held. Even with no one else in the shop to disturb them, the readers' low voices respected the peacefulness this shop seemed to ask for.

The scent of sandalwood, jasmine, and lavender tickled my nose. Crystals hanging in a glass case reflected the tiny lights above them. Past the wind chimes, just beyond a shelf of books, stood a case displaying Native American jewelry made by Earth Magic people – those who trusted the elements and worked with, not against, them.

Everything in this shop touched the chords of my nature. I'm not sure how I'd been able to deny who I was for as long as I did. Powerful chills raked my arms. Rubbing my hands against them seemed to make it worse, as if spirits were angry for being ignored for so long.

Alma, the owner, walked down the two steps leading to the main shop area. My mom mentioned her many times to me. Alma opened this place because she wanted Sandpoint to have access to books about the metaphysical and spiritual world. People were naturally drawn to the area, seeking answers to their life's questions. And Alma had them, or she knew someone who did.

"I'm just looking around," I said.

"Have you been here before?" Alma asked.

"No," I shook my head.

"Well, if you need anything in particular, let me know. There are more books in the back," she said gesturing behind her. She turned to the other side of the room and pointed. "We have a few new items in that corner. And here I have some wonderful bundles of sage and lavender from a local woman."

I breathed it all in. "I'm just going to look around a little."

Alma nodded and smiled again, walked toward the back room, and disappeared around the corner.

Actually there *was* something I wanted to learn about. Against the back wall, about halfway down, I found several books on Earth magic. I slid two from their place on the shelf and tucked them under my arm. On the way to the counter, I grabbed a box of oracle cards.

"Excuse me," I said.

Alma quickly got up and rounded the corner to the counter.

"Did you find what you were looking for?" she asked.

"Yeah, I did." I pushed the cards and books toward her. "Who can I see about clearing and moving energy?" I asked her.

"Like chakras or attachments?"

"Blocks," I said. "Life issues. I have some stuff I'm ready to let go, but I don't know how."

From beneath the counter she pulled out a Rolodex and flipped through the cards. She found the name she was looking for and wrote it on a piece of paper.

"Call him," she said, handing me the card. "His name is Shawn. He knows a lot about clearing and healing. That would be a good place to start." As she rang up the sale, she said, "You know, Solstice is the perfect time to set new intentions for yourself. It's a day to punctuate closure in some areas of your life, and also to celebrate the awakening of others." She shrugged. "Just something to think about."

Solstice. New beginnings. New me. It made a lot of sense. Returning her smile, I paid for the book and cards, then walked away, knowing I was about to do something I should have done a long time ago.

# CHAPTER TWELVE

I called Shawn right after I left Alma's shop. A sense of urgency pushed me to do this on the summer solstice because it *was* about new beginnings.

Shawn's house was on the other side of town, close to the Long Bridge and right across from the lake. His backyard, where he'd set up the ceremony, was drenched in sunlight that warmed the damp, green grass. There was an almost magical feel about it, and Shawn, with his long, graying hair, and the graceful movements of his tall, lean body, reminded me of a wizard from a mystical world.

I followed him as he walked around the yard, picking up sticks, discarding some and keeping others.

"The fire ceremony," Shawn explained to me, "connects us with Spirit and helps us release old patterns that hold us back.

"Basically we offer a sacrifice to the flames, and the vehicle for that sacrifice can be something like a letter or an object such as this."

"A stick?"

"Sure," he said, picking up another one. "Anything that you can pour your heart or thoughts into. We call this," he said, holding up the small twig, "a death arrow."

It sounded serious. But, damn, I was serious about moving on. From the sticks that lay around the yard, I chose a short, thin branch and broke it into a smaller piece, just as Shawn had with his.

"Is this okay?" I asked, holding my slightly tweaked, slightly knobbed choice of vehicle for him to see.

"Whatever works, as long as it feels right to you. The purpose of the death arrow is to carry our limiting thoughts into the fire. From there, the fire will transform and release that energy.

"For example," he said, kneeling next to the fire pit to begin preparing it for the ceremonial fire. "A very common belief is that we are not worthy of love, abundance, or success, so we put that energy out there and that continues to reflect back in the people around us."

He couldn't have hit closer to home. *I was not worthy of love. I was not okay.* That had been drummed into my head by my dad day after day. He'd told me that I should change who I was so I would fit in and be accepted by him and his church. So what did I do? I changed who I was in order to be loved. And the people I had surrounded myself with? Taylor and her posse.

I looked up and caught Shawn watching me. My face flushed hot. "I'm sorry. I kind of zoned out. What were you saying?"

"No, don't be sorry. It's good that you're giving this some thought. You don't have to pick only one. Whatever you want to release is okay. When you're ready, you blow it into the end of the stick, like this."

Holding the stick like a harmonica in cupped hands, Shawn closed his eyes, seeming to gather his thoughts along with his breath. Then he blew into it a few times.

Then it was my turn. *I am not worthy of love. I am not okay the way I am.* As I thought the words, I felt the pain. I let my emotions out through my breath, and with it, something more came through. Something much heavier, much more powerful rode the tail of my shame. It took me a few minutes to understand the emotion. My shaking hands could have been mistaken for fear or nerves, I suppose, but an overwhelming need to throw my death arrow, or anything else I could find, had me grinding words through my teeth. It was anger. Anger toward my dad for treating my mom and me like unworthy women, for trying to take our wings, for always being where he wasn't supposed to be… at the bar when he should have been home… at home when he should have been at the bar.

66

*Damn you, Dad! Damn you!* How freeing it felt to blow the top off my Pandora's box, and guide the thoughts into the stick. I hoped there would be enough room - because there was a lot of anger. My hands got tingly and sweaty, my head got light, but I couldn't stop. I didn't want to stop. I needed to purge the emotion that twisted a knot inside and held me back. A red hot acid burn welled up in my chest and forged a groove up my throat. I blew all of it into the death arrow. *I am not worthy of trust. I am not worthy of my gifts. And now, damn it... I release you.*

Shawn sat across from me, eyes closed, lost in his thought, fully engaged in creating his own offering. He seemed like such a happy, content, connected man. What could he possibly have in his life that would be consuming him the way it was? He seemed perfectly comfortable with who he was. I didn't see him running around town in bright colors with a trained smile on his face. He practiced what he believed in. It didn't matter who was watching. Like me. Staring. Peeking into his personal space. And it didn't bother him in the slightest.

A few more seconds passed before he opened his eyes and smiled at me. Not an embarrassed smile, like I would have probably given had he been watching me, but a genuine smile. Pure and simple. There's so much I could learn from him. Like my mother, he walked the walk and seemed at peace with who he was and what he believed in.

"So now we prepare the fire," he said, placing his arrow next to him.

"By placing two sticks in a Southern Cross formation in the center of the fire pit, it represents a point of navigation from the fire to spirit." He handed me some newspaper. "Help me wad up this newspaper and put them around the cross, like this." Then, using small, thin strips of wood, he arranged them to lean inward to form a teepee to direct the energy skyward.

Shawn lit the match and put flame to paper, which fed upon itself without hesitation, creating a mini-inferno within the teepee.

"I'm going to start a chant that will call upon the spirit of the waters beneath the Earth to help us." He paused, looking past my shoulder, his smile a mix of surprise and welcoming. "You've got ancestors here waiting to help you."

"Really?" I spun around, expecting to see the ghostly images of American Indians or Pilgrims, or even my grandmother. "Who?"

"I'm not sure." He cocked his head to one side, listening, his eyes fixed over my shoulder. "Family." He looked at me. "Can you feel them?"

Closing my eyes, I stilled my breath and mind. A soft breeze kicked up and the pressure behind my eyes intensified.

"I'm not sure what I feel."

"That's okay. Just know you have a lot of support." Out of a cloth bag, he pulled out an orange-sized bulb-kind of thing with engravings that created a band around the center.

"My rattle," he said, "and spirit water." He smiled and held up a small vial of liquid. "Spirit water honors the Spirits of the four directions when we call upon them to open the Sacred Space."

He shook the rattle and recited a beautiful chant in a language I didn't know. After sipping from the bottle of spirit water, he quickly blew it out in the four directions of South, West, North, and East.

The wooden sides of the teepee could no longer withstand the damage from the flame, and silently collapsed into a mound on top of the burned paper. I leaned closer and watched the exchange of give and take within the circle of fire.

"How often do you practice this ceremony?" I asked.

He used the handle of the rattle to push the burning pile around a bit. "At least once a month. It helps to rid myself of issues that don't serve my higher self."

The wood sizzled and the flame jumped to join the olive oil he drizzled across the pile. Shawn didn't take his gaze away from the fire as it settled itself into the bottom of the fire pit.

"Now we're waiting for the fire to become friendly."

"A fire can be friendly?" Definitely news to me.

He nodded. "When we have true intent and we resonate with the energy of the fire, then we can approach it without being burned."

Exactly what Mom had said, but I had a hard time believing I'd ever see fire the way they did. The images in my mind were still so vivid even after all this time – the flame snaking along the edge of the curtain, melting back the fabric to reveal a gaping flaw in my plan, punctuating its statement by dropping big-ass fiery exclamation marks onto the carpet. My frantic waving only fueled the fire to go faster and to get hotter, until it chased me out of my room and into my mother's, my screams echoing off the walls.

Shawn lightly touched my elbow, forcing me to get my head out of Illinois and back to Sandpoint.

"Do you see how the color of the fire has changed? The pattern of the flames is different, too."

I nodded, doing my best to see what he did.

"That's how you know the fire is friendly and ready to accept our offering." Shawn stood at the north side of the fire pit and said, "I'll go first. You can stand behind me and hold a space like this." His arms created a half circle to the sides and in front of him, like a protected harbor.

Wrapping the space around him was like wrapping my arms around a giant Sequoia. The centuries-old energy that surrounded him challenged the confines of my arms and pressed against my skin. Just like the ball of energy Mom and I had held in our palms, its vibration pulsed with heavy energy, testing my strength.

He kneeled in front of the pit and placed his death arrow in the heart of the flames. He then quickly passed his hands through the smoke and drew it toward his belly, again to his heart, to his forehead, and once more over his head, as if pouring the fire's energy over himself.

With his offering complete, he stood to face me. "Now you can approach from any direction."

I chose the west side and kneeled before the fire, with Shawn holding space behind me.

"Thank you," I whispered to my arrow, the holder of my secret pain, and placed it in the center of the fire with gratitude. I imagined the light of the energy within the arrow growing beyond its boundaries, wrapped in love, and being released into the air. Just as Shawn had done, I scooped the smoke from the pit and pulled it to my stomach, my heart, my forehead, and over my head. I waited for the cleansing energy to sink in before I stood.

In the pit, our sticks burned with such intensity I'd never seen before, as if they were gasoline-fueled. Sparks spit and the flames expanded and narrowed, not stopping until they had consumed our offering.

Before the fire could die down completely, Shawn handed me a slightly larger stick he had chosen earlier.

"This is the Pachamama stick. We blow blessings for the Earth into it."

Blessings for Mother Earth. I kicked off my sandals and pressed my bare toes to the grass, willing the vibration to connect with mine. I was now part of her healing and I would do whatever it took to help her. Pressing the Pachamama stick to my lips, I blew into the rough surface with true love and intent, and all my blessings, and then passed it onto Shawn. He closed his eyes for a moment before sharing his.

Together we placed it into the fire.

"Do you feel a difference in the fire now?"

The flames waved lazily as if they had all the time in the world to burn what was left of the wood. But I tried to see beyond the obvious. I tried to see with my soul instead of my eyes.

"The sense of urgency is gone," I said. "I sense calmness, like there's no more disturbance."

A smile tipped the corners of his lips up to mirror my own.

I felt like the fire. I found my moment of calm.

# CHAPTER THIRTEEN

My junior year at Sandpoint High School was a welcome change of pace. The rest of the summer had slipped by like a slow-moving stream – slow enough to enjoy, but not enough to go stir crazy. I spent a lot of time on our dock, reading the books I had gotten at the estate sale and learning more about myself.

Six months into the school year, I looked back and wondered how much longer I could have continued on in the role of the popular Alyx. Such a contrast. Since Taylor and I were no longer close friends, I completely faded from the social radar.

As for Justin, I couldn't compete with Taylor's determination to go back to him day after day to get his attention and, unless I joined the wrestling team, there was no hope of winning Justin over. The longer I watched him, though, it occurred to me that my competition wasn't Taylor after all. It was someone else he wanted. I had my suspicions about who it was, but the signs were too subtle to be certain.

I stood at my usual spot outside the school library's door, waiting for first period to start. Out of all the students who walked the halls, it seemed I was the only person who had changed since last year. The school was filled with the same students with the same attitudes.

Especially Taylor. Since the first day of school, she'd been back at it with Justin. For me, being on the outside looking in, Taylor's attempts to get Justin to talk to her were laughable. The way he side-stepped her constantly when she cut him off in the halls was, if nothing else, entertaining. That morning, though, it looked as if Taylor had taken a second look at Seth, who'd been walking beside Justin. Her expression almost... softened and she had... doe-eyes... but as Justin moved around her, not even acknowledging her, she snapped out of whatever haze she had gotten caught up in, and zeroed in on him again.

"I'll see you in class, okay?" Taylor spun around and called after Justin as he made his way down the hall.

Seth didn't seem to notice her either. But that wasn't a surprise. Even if Taylor had ever considered going after Seth, she definitely didn't stand a chance with him. He was in a serious long-term relationship with his girlfriend, Dani. No one could come between those two and as far as I knew, no one had ever tried.

But something was off about everyone in Seth's wake, because Taylor wasn't the only girl taking second glances at him. Necks strained to keep up with his pace down the hall, eyes begged for him to make a connection, and fingers touched lips, seemingly begging to be the next one kissed.

And he was clueless to all of it.

I pushed off the wall where I had been standing and followed Seth and Justin, making sure to stay hidden behind other kids. There was something different about the way Seth was moving. Or maybe it was just in the way he was carrying himself. More confident maybe. Less shy. In the last two years of watching Seth and Justin, their mannerisms and expressions were etched in my mind. Seth definitely walked with the cockiness of a guy who had just scored. But it wasn't in the way he walked that made the difference. It was in the energy he was putting off.

And, damn, if he wasn't magnetic. As if a cord connected us together, I walked faster to keep up. I had to get closer to see him… to touch him… to …

I hugged my body tight to break free of whatever had taken hold of me. I ducked into the next classroom - and bumped right into Justin. Staring at an eyeful of his indifference was almost enough to forget about Seth and his strange pull. Almost.

"Sorry," I mumbled, looking down so he wouldn't see the flush burning my face. I wanted to be anywhere else but

74

where I stood. If only I could hate him. That'd make my life so much easier.

I turned on my heel and stepped into the hallway. Checking to make sure Seth wasn't around, I headed to my locker.

A knife-edged coldness stabbed me in the chest and burrowed through to my back, stopping my lungs mid-breath. Adrenaline flushed my skin and sweated out my palms as I ran past Seth standing in the doorway of his classroom. There was no way I was going to make it to my locker. I turned and ran back down the hall and into the bathroom because I was close to losing everything I ate that morning. I leaned over the toilet and tried to slow down my breathing and thoughts.

What was going on with that guy? And what the *hell* just happened to me? Normally I wouldn't care about the other kids in this school, but when someone's issues had such a strong effect on me, I had no choice *but* to care.

# CHAPTER FOURTEEN

The fallout of seeing Jock Boy in the hall was intense and longer-lasting than I had expected. Considering I hadn't expected anything at all, the aftermath was over-the-top overwhelming.

After that freaky-ass encounter, I hid in the bathroom between classes to avoid seeing him. I was seriously creeped out all day. My senses were on high alert. It was as if something watched me, sniffing me out like a blood hound. There was a seriously dark force that pulsed strong, but somehow stayed contained within Jock Boy's body. I felt its threads winding around me, like tentacles reaching through bars. It was trapped. And it was evil.

Feeling a bit like a coward, I bolted out of the parking lot as soon as my last class got out. By the time I drove my car safely into my garage, though, I had convinced myself I wasn't running scared, merely staying one step ahead of something I knew nothing about.

~ ~ ~

"Well, was he angry with you?" Mom closed her book and placed it on the coffee table. "Maybe his negative energy was pulling you in."

It seemed to take forever for Mom and Jon to get home. After giving them a chance to settle themselves in, I rehashed what happened.

"I've never spoken to him," I said. "I don't think he knows I exist. I was just standing in the hall before my class. He didn't even notice all the other girls practically falling over themselves." I shook my head. "I've never seen anything like that before."

"If he wasn't aware of the magnetism… and Alyx felt a distinct pull…" Jon looked at Mom, "I don't know. Maybe an attachment?"

Mom dropped her gaze to the floor as she thought, and then slowly raised it to Jon's face. "That could very well be," she said. "It would have to be a strong attachment in order for so many others to pick up on the vibration, though." Her brows came together. "Highly unusual."

"Attachment?" I looked between the two of them. "Explain please?"

"An attachment," my mom said, "is an energetic body that enters an individual and disrupts his or her well-being. It feeds on the individual's energy."

"Like a leech." I shivered.

Mom nodded. "The signs can be so subtle that the intrusion often goes unnoticed, but left unchecked, the attachment can twist the individual's thinking and influence how he interacts with others. The host will often begin to behave just like the discarnate spirit."

"Seriously?" I sat in a chair across from her.

She nodded. "Most of the time the attachment's intentions are self-serving. Unlike our spirit guides who *give* to us from *outside our body,* an attachment *takes* from us from *inside our body.* If they're unable to let go of this energy plane," her arms made a sweeping gesture, indicating the space around us, "and cross the veil, they stay stuck here and oftentimes find a living, breathing extension of their residual issues. And since souls are energy, they follow the law of attraction. If we think sad thoughts, a sad soul is going to find its way in because they're drawn to us. If we're an addict, the drifter soul's toxic energies will only enhance what resonates within us. It's usually those with the most intense emotions that get caught up with an attachment."

"Well, there was definitely something off about him." I hugged away the goose bumps that colonized on my arms.

"It'd be a good idea to protect yourself," Jon suggested to me.

I looked at Mom. "How can I protect myself against something I can't see?"

"Well, there are different ways of going about it." Her eyes took in every detail about me. "It would help to wear brighter colors." Her hand shot up right away to silence the protest that had formed on my lips. "I said it would *help*. You might want to consider red lipstick to help gather some lighter energy." She cocked her head a little and smiled. "You'd look very pretty with red lipstick. Maybe a ribbon, but that's your decision. There are definitely other ways. Have you been centering yourself every morning?"

I nodded. That was something I loved to do. Every morning I flipped over the bucket I placed just beyond our patio outside, exposing a small patch of winter-dead grass. The stiff, stringy blades tickled the soles of my feet when I stepped onto the only clear patch of earth. I felt very much the Summer Princess when I pressed my toes into the frozen dirt, willing the energy from below the frosty surface to melt the layers between us. In much the same way I held energy for Shawn, I would reach out to the sides then to the front of me and encouraged the residual energy from my body to pool there before I released it to the air. I would lower my hands, and with slow exhalation, the energy poured out through my fingers and into the waiting earth. I filled the waiting space with white light, pushing the borders outside my body, expanding my personal space by at least six inches. I really didn't think that would be enough, though.

"I'm going to need more than light protection, Mom. When I followed Seth, something weird happened." I pointed to the center of my chest. "I felt it here. Like a string or wire or something had attached us together. Like a fisherman reeling in a catch. Or maybe the other way around."

"How did you untangle yourself from it?" Jon asked.

"By physically closing off. I crossed my arms across my chest and turned away. That broke the connection."

"Did you see Seth after that?" Mom asked.

"No way," I said to her. "I avoided him. I felt so out of control and sick to my stomach." I rubbed at my chest, erasing the phantom pull. "I know the centering and white light protection helps, but I want more than that. I don't want to take any chances." If Jock Boy had an attachment, I wanted solid steel shields to protect my body and mind.

Jon asked, "Do you know if he is going through anything major in his life? Something that might bring his threshold down?"

I shook my head. "I don't know much about him. Other than he's on the wrestling team and he's totally in love with his girlfriend, Dani."

"Well. Maybe the entity is just passing through," Jon suggested.

"Let's hope so." Mom and Jon clasped hands as if to show each other comfort. "I hate to see a young person have an attachment. The teen years are confusing enough as it is," Mom said.

Mom and Jon looked at each other and nodded as if a silent agreement passed between them.

"We could try a shield," Jon said turning to me. "It's simple, but effective. It'll block outside influences and prevent anyone from reading your thoughts or picking up your vibrations. Basically, you'd be shut off. The problem is that even though you'd be protecting yourself, you'll also be muting your intuition and senses."

"I don't want to go through what I did today ever again, and I definitely don't want to be its next target."

"That's perfectly reasonable," Mom agreed, "Especially now that you've been opening up."

Mom shifted to face me and took a cleansing breath, gesturing with her hands for me to do the same.

Jon grabbed a pillow from the couch and placed it on the floor in front of Mom. "You might be more comfortable," he whispered, gesturing to the pillow. He sat on the couch and looked to Mom for direction.

Positioning the pillow under my knees, I looked to Mom. Jon's encouraging nod helped me settle my mind and get focused on her instruction. Following her lead, I took three cleansing breaths. My focus went immediately to my core, right at my solar plexus, and I held it there until I felt the swell of energy expand.

Except for the gentle flow of our practiced breaths, the room fell silent. I gave myself to the rhythm of my heart and the slight tingling over the surface of my skin.

"To form your energy shield," Mom explained, "visualize the surface of it as being reflective. A mirror will not absorb negative energy, but will repel it back to its place of origin. Contain your aura within the shield so your emotions won't betray you."

White light filled the space beneath my heart, drifted up, then slowly enclosed it in a gentle blanket of heat. Slight tingling on my neck flowed upward to touch my face and head. My entire body hummed with pure energy and spilled over my physical boundaries. I was ready to do this.

Envisioning a one-way mirror, I muted the light within me and coated a reflective surface on the outside of my aura. My lungs tripped over the contained energy, as I breathed in my own light. I relaxed and allowed it to flow in and out, swirl around and comfort me. The boxed-in sensation gave way to a sense of free-floating. I then let go completely.

Jon was right. My senses were muted, but not as much as I thought. I could feel my mom's concern, or maybe it was just the way her brows tightened a little bit and the way she pressed her lips together.

"Well?" I asked.

My mom shook her head. "I'm not picking up anything."

"Then that's great, right?" I looked to Jon, but he looked her. "Why the concerned look then?" I asked.

"It's not concern at all. You're more powerful than you think you are. You put that shield up like a pro." The creases in her brow disappeared and her mouth softened into a smile. She leaned over and squeezed my hand, her warmth leaving an imprint of confidence and pride. "To take down the shield, reverse what you just did. Go slowly at first, but with time you'll be able to do it quickly."

I got up, expecting to feel as if layers of bubble wrap surrounded me, but it wasn't like that at all. The only indication that there was something between me and the outside world was a feeling of invincibility, with a little bit of vulnerability. But as far as Jock Boy was concerned, the slight decrease in my ability to fully sense things around me was a fair tradeoff for full protection against whatever he had going on inside him. Even if it was a harmless attachment, I would be ready.

# CHAPTER FIFTEEN

I practiced opening and closing the shield all weekend. The change in the sensitivity around me was more apparent each time. Mom and Jon did what they could to test me, but they didn't have the ability or experience to push me telepathically, as I suspected an attachment did. I *needed* to get this down because I didn't want to be caught off guard again. Until I discovered the reason for my reaction to Jock Boy, I wanted to be able to blend into the background unnoticed. I needed to buy myself time to study him. If his attachment was intent on hooking his claws into me, it'd better forget it. That so wasn't going to happen.

As much as this unnerved me, though, it was also kind of exciting. By opening myself up and embracing who I truly was, I had opened a portal to another world, another vibrational dimension, where harmony and disharmony co-exist, where people like me, Mom, and Jon, work to restore its balance. We were light-workers, and there was no way a simple attachment was going to trip me up.

~ ~ ~

As I got ready for school Monday morning, I convinced myself it would be a day like any other and for the most part, it had been. I psyched myself up for a big showdown all morning, but I never saw Jock Boy.

After lunch, though, I had Lit class with his girlfriend, Dani, so I'd definitely see him there. If he still had the attachment, I hoped to draw it out with a few focused thoughts. If he reacted – if *it* reacted – I'd let it get close enough to touch, but not close enough to get hold of me. The problem was, I wasn't sure if the attachment could somehow stop me from putting up the shield. Could it slide into my body against my will? My timing would have to be perfect.

Then again, all this planning could be for nothing. The attachment could have drifted off. Maybe what I experienced last week was a freak moment. Maybe I was giving myself too much importance in this whole thing. Maybe I was an innocent bystander. Maybe…

Without warning, pins and needles stabbed at the tips of my fingers and toes and shot up into in my chest, then crept up my neck, before engulfing my entire scalp. The urge to close off was nearly overpowering, but I held back and stayed open, sending out a beacon – only I wasn't so sure I wanted to hear his Polo to my Marco.

I looked at my phone. There were a few minutes before the bell would ring. I braced myself against a wall. It wasn't very long before he came into sight. There was a solid exchange – my energy for his – and Jock Boy was definitely feeling it. His shoulders stiffened and his brows scrunched above his eyes as they darted in and around the others in the hall.

He stopped mid-stride and spun to face me with an accusing glare distorting his face.

I pulled back my aura and locked up tight. My icy stare met his. *Heh. Not so tough, are you, my little parasitic friend?*

I felt prods and pokes, signs of its intention to break through. He felt me, which meant some of my energy was escaping the boundaries of my shield somewhere.

He wanted in. *It* wanted in.

From what I read about attachments over the weekend, this wasn't textbook at all. This one vibrated differently – a little darker, a little slower, like a base drum. Its pulse beat against my chest, in a slow, methodic rhythm. It was aggressive.

For now, my shield held. No hooks in my ribs, no breath-taking invasion of my body. I was relieved when Jock Boy turned his attention to Dani and walked away, taking his dark, creepy friend with him. I locked up my knees, afraid if I walked, my legs would give out.

That was freakin' crazy, but at least I know what I'm up against.

I think.

# CHAPTER SIXTEEN

Jock Boy knew I was there, and I was totally okay with that. I didn't care who noticed, even that dumb jock, Dirk. I knew he talked shit about me, but he was the least of my interests. My focus was entirely on Seth. From my spot against the back wall of the wrestling practice area, I scrutinized his every move. My presence irritated him - his scowls in my direction spoke volumes - but he couldn't do a damn thing about it. I wasn't about to walk away from him. He was amazing to watch. It was like he was on schizo overload, with chatter jabbing at his brain like a woodpecker. Every so often, his expression would slide away as if listening to something no one else could hear. But it'd be quick, then he'd look frustrated or pissed off - which was why this was so confusing to me. My mom and Jon told me attachments lay low, preferring to stay in the shadows, letting the host carry the legacy of their issues, but never really letting on that they're in there.

There'd been a definite change in Jock Boy, but it wasn't consistent. The vibes were dark and overpowering at times and other times his mannerisms were all Seth – unassuming wrestling stud, reserved, love-sick boy. It was like Dr. Jock Boy and Mr. Dark Soul.

There was something more, though … something … something dangerous. Soul attachments are flimsy. Their energy or power is not so great that they can't be released or chased off. This one, though, with the way it had settled into Jock Boy and the persistence it had been reaching out for me, was definitely not textbook.

Judging by the way Jock Boy looked at me each time I showed up at practice, it seemed I was getting on his stowaway's nerves. I wasn't buying into the animal magnetism thing and I sensed he, or it, would rather I minded my own business. But he didn't understand that it had *made* itself my business. That thing threw the first energetic punch. I couldn't let that go.

I was pretty sure Dani hadn't noticed it. At least it didn't seem like it. Every day she sat in the practice area doing her homework, without the slightest trace of concern.

Even if I wasn't able to feel it, and even if the attachment wasn't trying to get under my skin, I couldn't see how anyone could miss the changes in Jock Boy. Over the past few weeks, his shoulders and biceps filled out into freakin' cannonballs, and his body movements flowed with no effort at all. His reaction time had cut in half, as if he knew his opponent's next move even before they did. And just like a Secret Service agent, his eyes hardly stopped looking around, never focusing on a specific thing, always scanning the area for threats. His walk had taken on more than a swagger. It wasn't cocky at all. Cocky was arrogant and overly self-assured in a really obnoxious way. No. It's not that he tried to fake bad-ass. He *was* bad-ass. There was no question about it. Before this, he was shy and humble. A decent enough reason why so many girls wanted him. But now, even *more* girls wanted him. God help them all if he threw on some leathers and got a tattoo. All of those girls who flirted with him had no idea what they were flirting *with*.

Even if I hadn't been into Justin, I wouldn't have allowed myself to be affected by Jock Boy's magnetism. I couldn't let my guard down. I needed to figure *it* out before it figured *me* out.

Knowing what I did, and it wasn't much, I needed to give Dani a heads-up. It was obvious to me that her boyfriend had landed in some quicksand, and just how far or fast he might sink, I had no way of knowing until I had answers. I needed backup, and Jock Boy wasn't going to be very happy that I was about to recruit his girlfriend.

There was no easy way to approach this. I walked over to where she sat and started talking.

"He's got it bad."

"Who? What?" Dani looked up from her paper.

"Your boyfriend," I said. "I mean, I've been reading about it, and now here it is in front of me."

"What are you *talking* about?"

"You don't see it, do you? You don't see what's happening to him?" I leveled my face with Dani's and looked at her boyfriend, trying to see him from her perspective. Maybe the change in him wasn't as obvious to her as I thought it might be. If I told her what I knew, she'd probably think I was a complete nut case. I'd have to rethink how to approach her.

I straightened up. "Never mind."

"Hey!" Dani said. "What *are* you talking about?"

But I was already walking away. I took one last look over my shoulder at Jock Boy to see if he had been watching. Sure enough, his scathing glare was on me. I turned the corner and hurried down the stairs leading to the gym. I was halfway across the basketball court when Dani's voice slowed me down.

"Alyx! Wait up!" I stopped and turned around, and waited for her to catch up with me.

She seemed at a loss for words. We'd never really spoken to each other because, quite honestly, we had nothing in common. Even when I'd been popular, and we'd seen each other at the same parties, we hadn't ever spent any time together.

"About what you said up there." Dani found her voice. She tucked her hair behind her ear, exposing a small diamond stud.

"Um, listen," Dani stammered. "What were you talking about? What's wrong with Seth?"

I didn't say anything for a few seconds, still not certain how much I should say.

Dani shifted from foot to foot as if she couldn't contain her impatience.

"Who said anything was wrong with him?" I shrugged, giving me time to think.

"Well you did," Dani said. "Or at least you implied it."

I grabbed Dani's arm and yanked her toward me, taking two steps back.

"Hey!" Dani hissed. "What was that for?"

I pointed to the basketball that missed her head by a few inches.

"Sorry about that!" yelled a player on the court.

Dani turned and gave him a wave and a weak smile before turning back to me. "Thanks."

I shrugged and stayed silent, waiting for her curiosity to open her mind to what I had to say.

Dani crossed her arms in front of her. "Well? About Seth?"

I cocked my head to one side. Crossed arms. Yeah, not exactly open, but I tried anyway. "Haven't you noticed anything different about him?"

"What do you mean, different?"

I let out a breath. "Unusual, out of the ordinary, deviating from the norm."

"I *know* what different means," Dani shot back.

"Well?" I said. "Think. Have you noticed anything that's off about him?"

She huffed an impatient breath and shifted her weight. Her gaze flitted around the walls behind me as if she might find the answer.

"Well, he's been getting headaches and stomachaches lately," she said

"Seriously? That's all you've got?" I didn't mean for it to come out so harsh. I only wanted to get something more solid, but I didn't want to lead her with my own ideas. I wasn't exactly sure how much time we were dealing with.

She opened her mouth to say something, but stopped herself, her lips pressing into a tight line.

"I'm sorry," I said. "Is there anything else?"

She nodded. "The dogs at the shelter were acting funny around him. They wouldn't let Seth get close to them, like they were scared of him. Even his favorite dog backed off."

I grinned. Finally we were getting somewhere. Dogs were sensitive to subtle energy shifts. If they were suddenly uncomfortable being around Seth…

"What?" Dani asked. "Does that mean something?"

I started to answer, but movement at the railing upstairs caught my eye.

Seth stared down at us from the wrestling area.

Dani turned and followed my gaze. She turned back to me, her eyes wide.

"Meet me tomorrow after school," I said, barely moving my lips. "I'll be at Memorial Field. Top of the bleachers. We'll talk then."

I turned and made my way out of the gym, letting the door slam behind me, well aware of the two sets of eyes that were boring holes into my back.

# CHAPTER SEVENTEEN

I purposely chose to sit at the top corner of the cold, metal bleachers. From there I would have plenty of time to anticipate the energy of anyone who might show up, namely, Seth. I was pretty sure Dani wouldn't show up alone. I listened for voices or a second set of footsteps when I heard a car door slam shut. Without looking up from my book, I knew the light, quick footsteps in front of the bleachers and up the steps were Dani's. They sounded determined and anxious. And they planted themselves in front of me.

The smoke that escaped from the end of my cigarette curled like a serpentine around my fingerless black gloves before billowing out and disappearing into the air. Flicking the ash from the end of it, I took my time bringing the cigarette to my lips and taking in a deep hit. I decided to tell her what I knew. The more I thought about what Jock Boy was hooked up with, the more convinced I was that Dani and I could help each other. I needed to be careful, though. I had to be sure she could handle all of it. I closed my book and gestured for Dani to sit.

"I'll stand, thanks," Dani said, securing her backpack on her shoulder.

She seemed defensive, but at least she was curious enough to show up.

I shrugged. "Whatever. Suit yourself."

"So, what is this all about? Why all the secrecy?" Dani crossed her arms, but couldn't hide the slight tremors that shook her muscles.

"Your boyfriend's in trouble. I've been thinking—"

"What do you mean, he's in trouble? This is *Sandpoint*, for God's sake. Nothing bad *ever* happens here."

"I'm trying to help you," I snapped. "And believe me, you need help." I was a little on edge myself, not really knowing what to expect. I already knew I was in deep waters. I just didn't know how deep.

"If this is your way of trying to scare me, it won't work."

I couldn't help but roll my eyes. "Do you really think I have nothing better to do than to scare you?" I sucked in another lungful of smoke and took even longer letting it out. "What else have you noticed that has been different about him?" I asked again.

"Like I told you. The dogs at the shelter," Dani said. "They usually love him, but now they don't trust him. They won't get near him." She hesitated before adding, "Gracie, the woman in charge at the shelter, told Seth not to come back because the dogs were getting too disruptive."

Sensing a dam was about to break, I took a notebook out of my messenger bag and started to write. I didn't have to wait long.

"His eyes. His eyes are different, like they're darker or like there's smoke behind them. Shadows, maybe." She looked at me for a reaction, but I kept writing.

"Every time I ask him about it, he either changes the subject or turns away," Dani went on. "And the way he kisses me lately has been unreal."

"I'm not interested in your sex life," I said, looking up from my notes.

"No, I mean it's different. It didn't used to be this way. Now when he kisses me, it's like he's inside me and around me. He reaches places without even touching me."

She frowned, as if she were trying to understand.

"Explain please?" I said.

"But I can't," she said. "I've been trying to explain it to myself. Like once we were standing outside of my house, and it felt like he kissed me, but his lips hadn't even touched mine." Dani spread her arms helplessly. "I know it's lame, but I really don't know how else to explain it."

"Huh. Energy transfer," I said.

"What?"

"Energy transfer," I explained. "Relatively simple to do, if you're skilled enough. Healers. Reiki workers. People like that can do energy transfer." Definitely a possibility, but I was pretty sure Jock Boy wasn't into the healing arts.

She looked at me like I had lost my mind.

Okay. He definitely wasn't.

"What else?" I urged.

Dani took a deep breath. "Well, here's the one that bothered me the most. Seth didn't think I noticed, but at the time it really freaked me out. At the winter dance." Her brows came together as she remembered the details. "Dirk was trying to get me to dance and he made a grab for my elbow, but he stopped when Seth put his hand up. Dirk just... stopped." Dani gave a shaky laugh. "I've never seen Dirk so confused. It was like he couldn't help himself, like he *had* to listen to Seth."

So *that's* what happened. I remembered that, but from where I stood across the floor, I couldn't see what went down. "Anything else?"

Biting her lip, Dani sighed. "He gave me these earrings," Dani tucked her hair behind her ears, giving me a moment to see them again. "After I put them on, it was so weird. One minute I was telling him that he shouldn't have bought them and the next thing I knew we were kissing. I didn't remember standing close enough to kiss, but there he was. My mom was in the next room and normally I wouldn't kiss him if she was nearby..."

I nodded and glanced away. "Amazing," I said. It was one thing for an attachment to muddy up the host's thinking, but could it reach beyond its physical boundaries? "Amazing," I said again.

"What's amazing?" Dani asked. "Tell me. What's amazing?"

"Have you noticed he's gotten bigger?" I said, steering away from the possibility of such an aggressive and perhaps powerful attachment. Instead I spread my hands to show Seth's shoulder width.

"Yeah, but he's working out a lot." Dani stopped, seemingly struck by an awful thought. "You think he's doing steroids, don't you? No way. He'd never do something like that."

I shook my head, shaking off pressure building against my temples.

"No, I doubt it. But you have to admit that he's putting the other guys down on the mat with no problem these days."

"Wait a minute." Dani looked at me suspiciously. "How do you know so much about his wrestling?"

Sweat trickled down my back and my scalp started tingling. I kept my eyes steady and focused on her face. "I've been watching him."

Dani's eyes narrowed.

Could she seriously think that I wanted him? *Pfff.* "Relax," I said, closing my eyes against a sudden headache. "Dark, angry, possessed jocks aren't my type." *Crap!* I didn't mean to say that, but the need to protect myself overruled the need for caution. Inside my mind I took two steps back and put up the shields. The pressure behind my eyes was intolerable.

Dani's jaw dropped. "Uh…possessed?"

"Well, well, well. Speak of the devil himself." I looked past Dani, down to the bottom of the bleachers.

Jock Boy had found us. Not surprising in the least.

Dani whipped around and gasped. "Oh, shit."

Me? I was ready. I was used to the sensations that crawled over my skin when he was around, but not usually this intense. That was the very reason why I had positioned myself so far up the bleachers.

Jock Boy took the steps two at a time. Too fast, but not faster than I could buckle my bag shut, my notes safely inside. He stood next to Dani, using his height to try to overpower me.

I countered his gaze with mine, not once looking away. I wasn't intimidated by either of them.

Dani wrapped her arm around his waist, acting as if the tension between us wasn't a big pink elephant in our cozy little living room. "Hey, babe! How'd you know I'd be here?"

He shrugged off her question, and kept our eyes locked. "Aren't you going to introduce us?"

I took another hit from my cigarette and blew the smoke in his direction. Out of the corner of my eye, I saw Dani look from Seth to me and then back to Seth, her eyes blinking under a frown.

"Seth, this is Alyx from my Lit class. Alyx, this is Seth."

"How's it going?" he asked.

Yeah. Like he cared. I wasn't going to tell him shit. Besides, I was busy looking for a way inside of his head, but it seemed he had his own defenses in place.

"Nice to finally meet you." I said. "I gotta go." I nodded at Dani. "We'll talk later."

"Okay. Yeah, sure," Dani said, her voice trailing off.

I slung my bag over my shoulder and headed down the stairs. Neither of us was going to give in. The question was, who was going to make the next move?

With all that I'd learned from my mom, what I'd been researching, and who I was, I knew I could handle Jock Boy. Though obviously not a textbook situation, the basic rules were the same across the board.

But apparently those didn't apply to him. He was above that. In the next couple months, Jock Boy made it very clear he wouldn't play by the rules.

Even if it meant good people could die...

# MY SINCEREST THANKS...

It's never completely easy to go from *Once upon a time* to *And they lived happily ever after (or not)*, but the road down that path is less lonely when a writer has the encouragement of friends and family. While writing *Soulstice*, I had an amazing support team behind me, keeping me going all the time. My cousin, Maria, summed it up well: "I may let you rest a little, but I won't ever let you give up." None of them did.

I want to thank those who were the eyes and ears I depended on over the last year: Cassia Pabis, Maria Quezada, Toria Melendez, Natascha Troehler, Angela Peart, Fabio Bueno, Kathleen Mulroy, Shainnie Wade, and Theresa Renner (who made sure my I's were dotted and T's were crossed).

A special thanks and congratulations goes out to Alicia Schnell, whose editing skills of *Soulstice* earned her an "A" on her high school senior project. Way to go, Alicia!

Again, my sincerest thanks to you all.

Cover Photographer: Victoria McCune
Cover Design: Crystalynn Abercrombie
Model: Wrenee
Make-up: Kimberlee Langford

## AUTHOR'S NOTE

Thank you for reading *Soulstice*. When Alyx first made her appearance in *Souled*, all I knew was that she was going to be a Goth-type character, the complete opposite of Seth's girlfriend, Dani. Her attitude was sassy, tough, and nothing seemed to shake her confidence. I knew her character would grow in the next novel of this trilogy, but what I hadn't expected was readers, as well as me, wanting to know what made Alyx who she was. So I dug a little deeper into her past, and *Soulstice* was waiting to be written. Alyx needed her spotlight, if only for a little while.

I invite you to sign up for my newsletter at www.dianamurdock.com (click on "Let's Talk") to receive news about sales, new releases, and other fun news. Don't worry, though. I won't flood your email box with unnecessary stuff.

As a writer, I encourage any comments you might have. I would very much appreciate it if you would take a few minutes to leave a review on Amazon and let me know your thoughts. If you do, please email me at dianamurdockauthor@gmail.com with a link to your review so I can thank you personally.

Thank you again for spending your valuable time with the teens from Sandpoint, Idaho. My next project in the Souled Series… Justin's and Alyx's story.

### Where I hang out when not writing…

Website: http://www.dianamurdock.com/
Facebook: https://www.facebook.com/pages/Diana-Murdock-Author/114706771907294
Twitter: https://twitter.com/Diana_Murdock
Pinterest: http://pinterest.com/dianadmurdock/

www.ingramcontent.com/pod-product-compliance
Lightning Source LLC
Chambersburg PA
CBHW070223140626
46555CB00018B/1250